DREAM OF THE BLACK BUTTERFLY

# About the Author

Mark James Barrett is a freelance writer, author and screenwriter.

He graduated from Sheffield Hallam University in 2011 with an MA in Creative Writing and has since been short-listed for the Impress Prize for New Writers and the International Aeon Award Short Fiction Contest. *The Dreams of the Black Butterfly* is his first book. He can be found at markjamesbarrett.com.

Mark lives in West Yorkshire with his wife Victoria, their daughters Lara and Isabella, and a nervous cat called Dorothy.

*for Sharon,*

# THE DREAMS OF THE
# BLACK BUTTERFLY

*Best Wishes*

*Mark Barrett*

MARK JAMES BARRETT

Matador
9 Priory Business Park,
Wistow Road, Kibworth Beauchamp,
Leicestershire. LE8 0RX
Tel: 0116 279 2299
Email: books@troubador.co.uk
Web: www.troubador.co.uk/matador
Twitter: @matadorbooks

ISBN 978 1785890 543

British Library Cataloguing in Publication Data.
A catalogue record for this book is available from the British Library.

Printed and bound in the UK by TJ International, Padstow, Cornwall
Typeset in 11pt Aldine401 BT by Troubador Publishing Ltd, Leicester, UK

Matador is an imprint of Troubador Publishing Ltd

*With love*

*for*
*Henry and Frances Barrett*
*who have always believed*

*"Our life is no dream, but it should and will perhaps become one."*
*Novalis*

# Iquitos, Peru

## September 8th 1926

The doors of Cavendish House opened just after dawn, as the mournful call of the Common Potoo drifted through the mist. Lamps flared behind the shuttered windows, dimmed a little as they were adjusted, and began floating through the rooms of the big house under unseen hands. The sizzle of bacon on a skillet and the smell of coffee, murmured instructions growing louder. As the sun cleared the treetops, it was as though Pachamama herself was drawing the mist back into the jungle with a slow intake of breath.

A steady stream of tea chests and rough wooden crates were brought out and deposited on the gravel drive. Horse-drawn carts began to arrive from Iquitos Town. They queued beneath the giant trees, waiting to be loaded. The men got down, watered their horses and stood beside them smoking cigarettes in the warm, green shadows.

Alice Cavendish watched it all from the bottom of the long, sloping garden. For an hour she had been slumped over an iron table, chin resting on her folded arms, eyes following the labourers and servants as they went back and forth through the entrance to her home. Occasionally, she would hear a shrill cry from her mother upstairs, demanding something be done more quickly, more carefully, and yet the labourers seemed indifferent to her demands. They moved with a languor befitting the rising temperature.

The previous Christmas, Alice's father had brought back a steel toy from England. It was a Noah's Ark, almost as big as Alice herself. When the handle was wound, Noah, his family and the pairs of animals would clank along on a chain system, enter the bow of the ship, then reappear at the other end and go around again. At regular intervals, a tiger and a whale would pop up at the tiny windows.

Alice's house reminded her of that toy now; somebody, God maybe, was turning a handle very fast and had been all morning.

Despite what her parents had told her, Alice had never believed any of this would actually happen.

She got to her feet and stretched her arms. The sun was almost above them now and her layered dress was soaking up the heat. As she wiped her brow and looked around the garden, she saw the butterfly net lying beside the long rows of her mother's prize orchids. Alice walked over and picked up the net. She moved with quiet deliberation along the perfectly tended border, trailing the net through the flower heads then slashing at them with vicious snaps of her arm. Large, torn petals fell around her like discarded handkerchiefs. The vandalism improved Alice's mood for only a few moments. She turned her attention to her nurse, Lizzie, who was watching the Indian men haul crates onto the horse-drawn carts. Alice crept up and gave the young black woman a whack on the elbow with the handle of the net. Lizzie spun around, a mixture of pain and shock on her face.

Alice smiled. "You are paid to attend to me, Lizzie, not lust after men – Peruvian men at that."

Lizzie glanced back at the house. Mr Cavendish was watching from the study window, his whiskery jowls wreathed in pipe smoke. "I was not … Where did you learn that word anyhow, child?"

Alice slumped to the dusty lawn, which had been left un-watered since the decision to move had been announced. She sighed, began tapping the ground beside her with the net, and then tossed it aside.

"I know lots of words ..." She lifted her chin and gave Lizzie a contemptuous look, which quickly crumbled. Her eyes filled with water. "It's not fair!"

Lizzie knelt and took her hand. "Life ain't supposed to be fair. But your new home in Malaya, well, it will be just as fine as this one ... finer I heard." She stroked the back of Alice's hand for a few seconds, and then stood up. "Come along; get up from there now or the ants will have your buttocks for lunch." She smiled in encouragement. It was customary at this point, for Alice to mock the way Lizzie pronounced the word 'buttocks', with so much emphasis on the second syllable.

Alice got to her feet slowly. Tears continued to pulse down her cheeks, but now there was a thoughtful look on her face, as if she was wrestling with something. "I'm accustomed to far greater invasions. Father ... he ..."

From the house there came the crack of a whip and the slow crunch of displaced gravel as another load headed for the docks.

Lizzie took the girl's arm and turned her away from the house. "You mind your tongue now, and be careful where you wag it." But her tone melted quickly, and she put her arm around Alice, pulled the girl's head into her stomach and stroked it.

"He comes to me at night." Alice said. She began sobbing into Lizzie's apron.

Lizzie looked back at the house in alarm, fearful the words had carried somehow. Her own eyes began to fill. "Oh Jesus, that's why he tired of me," she whispered. "I am so sorry honey, but he has rights over you and me, all of us here. It's a burden we have to carry, only God knows for why."

Alice gripped Lizzie's waist tighter still. "And now I have to travel halfway across the world with him!"

"Oh my Lord," whispered Lizzie, looking over Alice's shoulder. "Would you look at that?"

Alice, startled by the change in Lizzie's voice, turned to see what had caused it. Sitting not 10 feet from them was the biggest, blackest butterfly she had ever seen. It was resting on the pacay tree at the very end of the garden, balancing on the tip of a giant palm at head height. Alice got the impression that the creature had just alighted there as she turned, because the palm branch was swaying slightly in the still air. The butterfly opened and closed its wings slowly and they flashed with a rich darkness.

"Goodness, it's enormous!" Alice wiped her eyes and walked towards it. She reached up to the creature and tentatively pushed her fingers under its head, hoping it might sit on her hand. The black butterfly's furled proboscis twitched and Alice noticed the glossy hairs around its bulbous eyes. The wings opened for a moment and then closed, each of them as big as the fan her mother cooled herself with when she sat in the parlour each evening after dinner.

Lizzie joined her. "Be careful there, honey."

"It tickles," Alice said, a shiver running over her sweating skin. She giggled as the creature edged onto her hand and settled there.

"Where did you come from?" She asked, as if she were petting a puppy.

Alice felt a sharp jab in her palm, and whipped her hand away. "Ow!" She cried, stumbling backwards, shaking her arm in shock. A light-headedness overtook her quite suddenly. The butterfly's wings opened again, stretching wider and higher until everything else seemed to be blotted out. Alice felt like she was falling into them …

Vaguely, she heard Lizzie calling up to the house for help and people shouting her name. There was a blur of movement as one of the gardeners passed her with a machete and cleaved the butterfly almost in two, across the wings and through the abdomen. It fell to the floor with the palm branch beneath it and lay twitching feebly at Alice's feet. Her father caught her in his arms.

"Alice! Alice! What happened?" he asked breathlessly. The thick smell of tobacco filled her nostrils and she wished the butterfly had taken her away.

"It bit me, Father. I think it bit me." Alice held out her hand to show him the puncture mark on her palm. As he took hold of it, she looked up and saw eyes watching her from the trees just beyond the end of the garden. They were human eyes and just as quickly as she had registered them, they were gone.

★ ★ ★

*I eventually found the Quechua Indian who had started all these rumours about three days down the Rio Maranon, in a tiny village that had probably never had a name. My guide, an indolent Mestizo I'd procured in Iquitos, located the individual after much prevarication by the locals.*

*I can assure you, I am not a man for melodrama, but there was a terrible atmosphere in that little hut; the smell was ungodly, the air a soup of mosquitoes. I caught but a glimpse of the butterfly in question, laid out on a rough, wooden table in the corner. The Yagua Indians, four of them, shuffled around it as we entered. The insect was large, easily two feet across the wings, and black as a jungle night.*

*He was slumped against the wall, a tiny man whose eyes looked neither at us nor past us, but seemed to be turned in upon himself, watching perhaps, as his mind slid slowly off the edge of the known world. My guide tried to get him to speak for nigh on an hour and I had just about given up on the whole enterprise.*

*I remember saying, "The fellow's beef-witted; we will get nothing from him," but it was clearly worse than that.*

*Then, quite without warning, he began talking.*

*"Well?" I asked my guide when he had dried up.*

*"He says that he took the black butterfly from the forest, near this place, that it bit him."*

*"Bit him? Preposterous! What else, man?"*

*"He says only that there are stories in the wings."*

*I tried to get more of course, but we were ejected soon after and there was nothing for it but to head back to Iquitos.*

*I don't think I shall ever forget the man's eyes, and those words he kept repeating.*

*"Hay historias en las alas." There are stories in the wings.*

*Extract taken from Following the Amazon, William Musgrove,*
*1834*

## The Pacaya Samiria National Reserve, Peru

## October 2nd 2006

An unearthly roaring rolled through the treetops of the Pacaya Samiria National Reserve, waking Moises Quispé from a shallow, fitful sleep. He pulled back the mosquito net and lay shivering for a few minutes, listening to the branches high above him rattle violently as troops of howler monkeys disputed territorial rights. Large, dew-wet leaves sailed down from the frenzy and slapped against the roof of his tambo. Moises pulled the thin pillow around his head and began humming into it, hoping to drift back into sleep, knowing it was futile.

He gave up after a few minutes and swung himself out of the hammock, grunting like an octogenarian who begrudges struggling through one more day of life. Half asleep, he moved across to his lookout chair, noticed a vicious looking bullet ant had found its way in and crushed it beneath his boot. His blank eyes reflected the mist as he sat back and pulled the blanket from the hammock to cover his legs.

The discordant opera echoing through the forest grew steadily louder as the mist dissipated. Moises knew dawn's arrangement by heart; it was the soundtrack to his life. Sometimes he wished for a moment of peace and felt guilty for the wishing. The rituals he was listening to had been practiced unbroken for millions of years, so why should they pause for him? The eight years he had spent adding his own communion had seemed much longer: reciting the same prayers every morning and repeating the same movements. In the steaming darkness outside the tambo, those creatures he honoured had always seemed oblivious to his ministrations.

Moises stretched his arms with a sigh and took a gulp of

water and a handful of grubs from his backpack. Occasionally he raised his binoculars in response to movement outside the hut, the flutter of a parrot's wings perhaps or a peccary rooting around for its breakfast on the gloomy forest floor.

His mind, starved of new experience, circled around the same old subjects, like a condor returning to bleached bones in hope: Hawthorne ... the black butterfly ... and Señor Dollie of course. Moises turned the improbable figure over in his mind again: one million Nuevo Sol to anyone who captured the elusive black butterfly. But the chances were so small. He had been moving from one tambo to another for half of his life and had not even caught a glimpse of the creature. The little hut in which he sat was tambo number six; every one of them looked the same, felt the same, and *la selva* was vast. It was his love of *la selva* that sustained him, but his heart felt as black as he imagined those wings to be. He had to find the butterfly before anyone else did; yet he was so tired of looking that a growing part of him wished someone else would find it, just to release him from the dream of success.

His tutor Hawthorne had told him a secret the previous year in Iquitos: something Moises might not have believed had Hawthorne not disappeared soon after, vanishing like people sometimes did here – completely and without question or comment. The secret had sustained him so far, but with each empty day that passed, he began to doubt the truth of it.

By ten o'clock, the jungle had quietened and he felt himself drifting again, lulled by the heat and the monotonous purring of the cicada. Through his fluttering eyelids he registered movement far above him. Something large and dark was floating down from the canopy in a graceful spiral.

Moises stood up.

Beside the slow, obsidian swirl of the river were a number of puddle clubs: groups of butterflies sitting with their wings folded, like clusters of miniature yachts littering a muddy shore at low tide. They gathered there every morning to suck the minerals and salts from the moist soil. A black shape had settled among them.

Moises leaned forward to part the netting, brought his binoculars up and fumbled to adjust them.

"I see you," he whispered, and flakes of dried mud fell from his cheeks as he smiled.

The sounds of the rainforest receded. A cold pulse of sweat broke on the boy's skin and his belly began to crawl; the ghosts of the catfish he had eaten the previous evening circling inside him. *Was it true?* Finally confronted with the creature, he realised that he had never truly believed in its existence before this moment. To his weary eyes it appeared more solid, more real than everything around it, and yet so black it might have been a hole in the jungle, a fluctuating glimpse into another world.

"*Exquisita,*" Moises murmured. He ducked through the mosquito net in a fluid movement, his eyes never leaving the quarry as he gently teased the telescopic net from his back sling and began to extend it.

The black butterfly was less than fifty feet from his hide. Moises halved that distance in a matter of seconds, treading softly between the groups of twitching butterflies, his breath coming fast and shallow. A few of the insects rose into jittery flight and he paused. The black butterfly was completely still, detached from it all, like a rare god fallen to earth. Moises moved his feet again, much more slowly now, but the disturbance spread. Soon delicate clasps of colour were flickering all around him. He noted a few of the species whose names had been drummed into him these past few years: the clear wings of *Greta oto*, flashes of rich orange from a *Dryas iulia* drifting into sunlight, blood red and sky blue from members of the *Nymphalidae* family, and the yellow, leaf-like *Pieridae*.

9

Moises was within 10 feet when the black butterfly finally reacted to all the commotion. It opened its velvet wings and slowly lifted from the ground. He broke into a run, instinctively swinging the net in a great arc to overtake the creature as it rose towards the safety of the canopy.

"*Pachamama!* I have it!" Moises cried in disbelief, as he pulled the net towards him and fell to the ground, holding it down so the butterfly could not escape. He unscrewed the long pole and tossed it into the undergrowth. "I have it!" he repeated. It was unbelievable. He looked around as if to find someone to verify what had just happened. He shook his head, laughed a little, felt a scream rising in his throat. The insect began to flap so he held the net a little tighter, cooing as if he were tending to a fussing infant. Moises pulled out the other half of the capture net from his shoulder bag and slid it under the open end of the net between ground and butterfly. He snapped the catches on the frame and sat back. Tension left him in a shaky sigh.

Behind him, the other butterflies settled back to the mud and the noises of *la selva* seemed to resume the usual pattern in his ears. The giant insect in his net had folded its wings and was still, as if finally accepting its capture. Moises pulled at the net to give the creature some room to move inside. He stared absently into the trees for a moment and shook his head. What he had done was sacrilege. What he intended to do was even worse. There was a prepared syringe in his bag. He gripped the butterfly's wings gently between the thumb and forefinger of his left hand, and with his right, pushed the syringe through the net towards the creature's abdomen. His thumb hovered behind the depressor. Moises had never considered this moment in any detail before now, maybe because he hadn't really believed it would come to pass. Now, he realised that his heart didn't seem strong enough for such a crime against *Mama Selva*, even if it might be for the good of the jungle in the long run.

With a grunt he willed himself to push down his thumb.

He was paralysed. He just couldn't. He needed more time to think.

As he was removing the syringe from the net, his head filled with a mixture of relief and failure, a huge, hollow crack resounded through the forest behind him. He dropped the net and turned just in time to see a 60-foot barrigona tree cut his tambo in half. The walls opened like a V and collapsed as the splintered roof beams spun away in all directions. A cloud of bark dust and dry leaves rose from the impact and hung in the air for a few moments. From beneath the wreckage there was the feeble cry of something trapped and dying and then a relative quiet descended upon the area. A spider monkey came out of the mess, moving along the fallen trunk cautiously. It gave Moises a quick glance, skipped onto a nearby tree and ran back up to the canopy.

Moises stared at the destruction. If it had fallen ten minutes earlier, he would have been under there, a banquet for the ants. What did it mean? He lowered his head and closed his eyes, muttered a brief prayer. When he opened them again he turned quickly, picked up the net and gripped the butterfly as he had before. Before his nerve faltered, he pierced the insect's thorax and emptied the ethyl acetate solution into it. The butterfly flapped frantically in response and Moises felt a sting in his hand; he had been scratched by the net or the insect somehow. He sat down on a tree root and sucked at the nick in his thumb. The insect became still.

"*Lo siento mi hermano*," Moises whispered and his mud-caked face soaked up the tears like a dry riverbed.

On the journey back to the boat, his thoughts were consumed with one thing: examining the butterfly to check it was as special as Hawthorne had heard. But the microscope was far away.

The sweat bees swarming around his boots finally dispersed as he approached the banks of the Yanayacu. Moises took off his cap and scratched his sweat-drenched head as he surveyed the darkening sky. During the past week the bloated clouds, split by lightening, had gushed short, heavy bursts on *la selva* as if warning of the coming deluge. The rains were late this year. They would be here soon.

He stepped into the canoe and scanned the far bank, picking at the shadows for any danger. He saw only a flock of nunbirds and the solemn, white face of a monk saki studying him from high in the trees.

It would feel much safer on the river; at least he could see what was coming out there. He put on his sunglasses and took out the CD Walkman that Hawthorne had brought him back from Lima. He had three CDs, two that Hawthorne had bought him from a second-hand shop and one he had been given by Miss Gallo. Moises took them from his backpack and chose the one with Mary Poppins on the cover.

Moises fired the engine, guiding the light, long boat out onto the dirty water and the orchestra began to play in his ears. The jungle's green walls rushed past him and he sang along to the music in a spirited falsetto, guessing at the lyrics. Soon, the narrow river opened out and a lake appeared on his right. Pink river dolphins played at the inlet and a cloud of brilliant-white egrets took flight at the buzz of his 55 HP motor, flying right across the bow of the aluminium vessel.

It was two hours before he saw any humans. A motor launch filled with illegal loggers passed by, heading upstream. The men gazed at him impassively, chainsaws and guns resting casually in their laps. It was rare to see them at this time of year. They worked mostly during the rainy season when more of the reserve was accessible, cutting the rare cedar and mahogany and sending huge barges of logs down the rivers to be sold overseas.

Most loggers were so heavily armed that the rangers were reluctant to challenge them. Besides, this was *la selva de los espejos* – the jungle of mirrors: an ancient maze of rivers and vast lakes that was impossible to police properly, even if someone had wanted to. Moises had noticed that in the last couple of years, the loggers had seemed bolder and more frequent with their incursions. Sometimes, when at one of his posts, he would hear their chainsaws and the hate and frustration he felt crippled his thoughts for a while.

He reached the wider water of the Rio Samiria and felt a surge of hope course through his body. Maybe he would make it after all. Occasionally he passed river taxis or other boys under the employ of Emerald Earth. They chugged along in their llevo-llevos, raising their hands in greeting as he did, like a reflection across the water. He changed the CD in his Walkman, switching to Stevie Wonder, and pushed the boat harder, watching the prow slice through the white glass that stretched ahead of him. *I must make Prado by nightfall,* he warned himself. His thoughts died in the heat, boiled away until there was just the bitter concentration of his fear: Señor Dollie.

It was fear that told Moises to push on to Iquitos, to catch a flight to anywhere and find the safety of distance before studying the butterfly. But he could never leave *Mama Selva. Hadn't she given him life? Didn't her trees still embrace his family's spirits?* The boy's hand shook on the tiller as he guided the boat around the logs spinning slowly in the deep current. He considered his options. The only chance to look at the creature would be at Prado, where he had Hawthorne's equipment to hand.

*Why not just take it to Dollie and collect the reward?* The question skipped into his mind before he could stop it. *What difference would it make?* Hawthorne was gone, his brother, his parents … Moises turned his head and spat violently into the passing water. He fished in his shorts and pulled out a matchbox, took out the used piece of gum inside and popped it into his mouth, chewing loudly. He immediately felt a little calmer.

He would not give the black butterfly to Dollie.

And he would not run.

Iquitos still tempted him, though. Moises longed to be back at the Plaza de Armas, buying an ice cream cone from the *heladería* then crossing the road to eat it in the cool mist from the fountain. Yet another ritual, formed during meetings with his tutor Hawthorne, a gringo twice his age, who had originally come to Peru during the gold boom of the mid-nineties. Hawthorne was a tall, bony man with thick, curly, red hair and very pink skin, which never adjusted to the sun. He always smiled too quickly when other people spoke, as if he knew much more than they did and their ignorance amused him. The smile he used for Moises was quite different.

It was almost a year to the day that Moises had met the Englishman in Iquitos for the last time. They met on the main street of the waterfront, the Malecon Maldonado, their greetings lost in the growl of hundreds of three-wheeled moto-cars. The pitiless sun was almost at its height, fermenting the thick, grimy air beneath the colonial ironwork of the buildings. Hawthorne took Moises to the 'Dawn on the Amazon Café' for an early lunch. They sat at a small table under the large, white awning outside.

"The burgers are very good here, why don't you try one for a change?"

Moises nodded vigorously, his head down over the menu, as if the decision would be tough and needed much consideration.

"It's your lucky day, Mo," whispered Hawthorne.

Moises looked up as his favourite waitress arrived to take their order.

"Good morning, Gabriella. How are you today?"

14

The young girl gave Hawthorne a thin smile and took out her pen. "Good, thank you. What can I get for you?"

Moises watched the beads of sweat trembling on the swell of Gabriella's cleavage as the Englishman ordered. When she turned to him, he looked down and muttered his order. "*Tacacho con cecina por favor.*"

Hawthorne shook his head in disgust. "How long have you worked here, Gabriella?"

"Three years."

The Englishman leaned across and patted Moises's hand on the table. "You hear that, Mo? Three years." He leaned back and gave the girl one of his infuriating smiles. "That's a long time."

"I will be leaving in the spring," she said quickly.

Moises looked up.

"Where to?" asked Hawthorne.

She pointed out into the sun-bleached sky. "*La luna.*"

Hawthorne sat up. "Really? For one of the mining companies?"

She nodded.

"But what will you be doing up there?"

Gabriella put her pen back in her breast pocket. "I don't know. They tell me when I get there."

"I think we know what she will be doing," Hawthorne remarked as the girl returned to the kitchen. He turned to Moises. "You are running out of time with that one, Mo." And when he got no reply: "Bananas and pork again? You are just like those monkeys in the jungle, your routine never changes does it?"

She came back with two Iquiteña beers. Hawthorne chugged back half a bottle and burped loudly. He smiled. "Have you really never had a girl?"

Moises shook his head.

"You never will either if you don't speak to them. It is the first requirement."

As if to reinforce the point, Gabriella laughed as she took an order at a nearby table. Moises watched with a feeling of utter helplessness. His dreams were like tight knots in his chest, impossible to unravel.

The man and the boy finished their meal with a wedge of potent chocolate pisco cake and sat in silence for a while, content to watch moto-cars weave perilously through the dense traffic along the boulevard. Gabriella brought them beers whenever they ran low. Moises never tired of that wonder: an ice-cold bottle, its condensation dribbling over his fingertips.

At about two o'clock, a group of three men and one woman came into the cafe and sat down at the only large, six-seat table under the awning. Many people had tried to sit there since Moises and Hawthorne arrived and had been moved by the café owner. He appeared now and was very attentive to the group as he seated them. Only one of the men was Peruvian. The other two and the woman were gringos. She was as short as Moises and wore a loose, white blouse and khaki shorts, her brown hair cut in a bob. She removed her mirrored sunglasses as she sat down and smiled at the café owner.

Moises whistled quietly. Hawthorne had been watching the group, too. He turned and smiled at the boy.

"What's up with you?"

A man appeared from the street with a large camera and there was much discussion. Eventually he took a number of photographs of the group with the café owner, then some more of the woman on her own. The flash popped repeatedly, tiny lightning flashes under the awning's gloom bringing attention from the street.

"Paparazzi, Moises; we have the famous among us today it seems."

Things quickly quietened down when the photographer

left. The crowd of people at the entrance lost interest, not knowing who the woman was, and moved on.

"*Está muy buena*," Moises whispered; the table area outside was small and they were very close to the group.

"I don't know ... Do you think she is more beautiful than Gabriella?" Hawthorne shrugged. "You are invisible to both of them."

The famous woman had a sandwich and an iced coffee, and spent the next hour in deep discussion with the men at her table. One of the gringos seemed to be translating between her and the local. At one point, Hawthorne sighed and pushed his chair back. "Well, if you are going to stare at her all afternoon, we better find out who she is."

Moises made to stop the Englishman, but he was too late. He saw the shock on the woman's face when Hawthorne reached her table and when her big eyes met his, he looked down at the table cloth. He didn't look back up until Hawthorne returned.

"She is called Natalie and she is a South African pop star, here supporting a charity of some sort that helps women who lose their babies in childbirth. And she is even more beautiful close up, if you like that sort of thing."

By mid-afternoon, they were very drunk.

"Come on, let's go, Romeo." Hawthorne threw some notes on the table and staggered towards the street.

Moises followed reluctantly and as he passed the woman's table he turned his head away from it, feeling his pulse quicken. He heard his name and turned, thinking he had imagined the woman's voice making the shape of it. But he hadn't, she was out of her seat, moving around the table towards him.

"Hi, Moises," she said, holding out her hand. "Do you speak English?"

Moises blushed as he shook it. "Si, some English."

17

She laughed a little, showing straight, dazzling teeth and dimples formed on her cheeks. "Your father said you were a fan. Thank you so much."

Moises nodded. His tongue lay like a corpse in his open mouth.

"I wondered if you'd like this, if you don't have it already, that is?" She offered him a CD with her face on the cover.

Moises took it and looked into her eyes. They were grey-blue, like the sky in the moments just before dawn.

"Gracias … I don't, I mean thank you … gracias."

She laughed again and shook his hand. "Nice to meet you." As she turned away from him the sun caught her eyes and they flashed a clean, iridescent blue, now like the wings of a Blue Morpho.

The fountain at the Plaza de Armas was busy. The smell of Turtle stew and barbecued bananas swirled in the hot air, while bands played in the road, competing energetically for any spare centimos the tourists might have. The edge of the fountain was knotted with people eating ice cream. Above them, the street lamps hung like yellow fruit under a canopy of jagged palms. Moises sat at the water's edge, the cool spray peppering his skin, while Hawthorne stood over him making a scene. He flung out his arms.

"Moises loves this wretched island Iquitos, the only city in the whole godforsaken world you can't drive out of …"

Moises smiled half-heartedly, his thoughts elsewhere.

Hawthorne raised his voice. "… a city floating on the piss of its inhabitants."

"Si," Moises laughed, nibbling around the edges of his cone.

"You are the only boy I know who prefers the trees to the buildings, who prefers painting pictures to drinking. Me, I prefer to do both, which may explain the quality of my work."

"This is possible," Moises said.

The Englishman ruffled the boy's hair. "You have a little talent I guess, but you are no Chagall or Jose De la Barra." He sat and lit a cheroot carefully, before blowing a cloud up into the lilac sky. "Have you really fallen in love with that singer we met? I thought she was feeble-looking and far too old for you."

Moises smiled, his eyes flashing in the sodium light from the *heladería* across the road.

Hawthorne became serious. "Listen, I need your help with something."

"Okay."

"The Yaguas have a story about the black butterfly, don't they? You should know this; you are a bastard Indian after all."

Moises rolled his eyes. Hawthorne's cigar flared like sulphur in the dwindling light. "Tell it to me, not the tourist version … but the way your people understand it."

"Yana Wawa is a—"

"Yana Wawa? What does that mean? Black …?"

"*Hija* … erm …"

"Daughter?"

"Si, she is black daughter, a mountain spirit that went down into *la selva* thousands of years ago. She was punished for this; now she must serve *la selva* until the day when all the trees have fallen." Moises shrugged.

Hawthorne opened his hands. "Is that it?"

"It is said that if you capture Yana Wawa, she will tell you some great secrets about this world. But … if you listen, you must replace Yana Wawa and stay in *la selva* until it falls or until someone finds you and listens to your stories."

Hawthorne shook his head. "That's something like I heard." He looked around him quickly, as if scared of being overheard. "It's nonsense."

Moises threw away the rest of his cone. Something about

the way Hawthorne looked was making him nervous. "It is legend," he said, as if that explained everything.

"Could it be true?"

"Only Pachamama knows."

"I think Dollie knows, too, and he's a lunatic."

They sat at the kitchen table in Hawthorne's apartment just off the plaza and shared some marijuana. Hawthorne spent an hour telling Moises everything he had overheard about the black butterfly and then went through the books he had on microscopy.

"Take these with you tomorrow."

Moises found it hard to concentrate. It had been a long day and his mind was leaden from the weed they had smoked. It wasn't until Hawthorne whipped the piece of hessian sacking from the table and revealed a brand new microscope that Moises woke up a little.

"This cost many Sol," the Englishman said solemnly.

Moises had known Hawthorne for almost eight years; it was very unlike him to spend money without a great deal of thought.

Hawthorne began adjusting the instrument. "I am going to show you what to do."

"Why?"

The man stood up and leaned his backside against the table, his hands clasped in front of him. "One million Nuevo Sol is about three hundred thousand U.S. dollars. If what Dollie says is even half true, that insect is worth … Well, it's worth a hell of a lot more than that. Why not sell it to someone else?"

"But who?"

"I'm not sure yet?"

"But Señor Dollie–"

"Doesn't know I know. And besides, the odds of us finding it are small." Hawthorne offered the last of the joint to Moises and spat a shred of tobacco onto the floor. "I'm just a good boy scout. I like to be prepared."

Moises ran his fingers along the table top. "Will you leave me, Papa?"

The man pulled a face. "I'm not going anywhere. We'll work on the microscope in the morning. I'm too stoned for this shit."

Moises raised his head. "Tell me about your Luton again: the park, your friends, and the bar–"

"It's called a pub over there. The Old Moat House. I bet you know more about Luton Town than most Lutonians do." He giggled. "That is fucking bizarre when you think about it."

The giggles overtook him and Moises joined in, unsure as to what he was laughing so hard at. When the laughter dried up, Hawthorne took Moises's hands and kissed them. "Don't I deserve something first?"

A great roar of laughter came from the street and the music seemed to grow louder.

"Okay." Moises began to undo Hawthorne's bulging shorts.

"No, much as I love your mouth, I need to fuck you tonight."

Moises turned around dutifully and Hawthorne grabbed a fistful of his hair and pushed him over the sticky wooden table. His other hand pulled at the boy's shorts until they fell. Moises gasped as Hawthorne forced his way inside him. He felt Hawthorne's hot words against his neck as the man lurched and moaned.

"Oh Mo … you are my butterfly … my butterfly … What are you?"

"Bu … tter … fly …"

Moises watched the microscope next to his face shake rhythmically. As the pain of the Hawthorne attentions intensified, the black butterfly bloomed behind his eyelids.

A sudden cloudburst sent Moises scrambling around in the bottom of the boat. He covered the butterfly net with a tarpaulin and changed the CD in his Walkman. The river surface danced furiously until it blurred into the downpour, and sky and water became indistinguishable. Moises studied the CD cover as the rain popped against it.

"Natalie Gallo," he mouthed as the singer's anguished voice sent shivers of pleasure down his back. Moises put his chewing gum back in the matchbox and returned it to his shorts. He didn't believe that Hawthorne had chosen to disappear. It had to be Dollie's work.

*But why hasn't he come for me?*

Soon, the sun was out again and pulling steam from his clothes. Moises had reached Ranger Station Two at the mouth of the Rio Samiria. He was obliged to sign himself out of the reserve. Reluctantly, he cut his engine and glided up the channel that led to the pontoon. Little waves fanned out from his boat, sending undulations through the thick weed that flourished in the backwater. This was as quiet as *la selva* ever got.

Geraldo met him at the top of the wooden steps. "Had enough for this week?" He asked good-naturedly.

The other ranger, Luis, was asleep on the bench at the back of the room. His snores drifted out to them. Geraldo watched Moises sign the book and offered him a cup of water.

"What would a *Chibolo* do with all that money anyway?"

"What money?"

"The one million … if you found that stupid butterfly?"

Moises handed him back the empty cup. "I … I would save *Mama Selva*."

Geraldo laughed. "Would you? Don't you want to see the world, get away from those chiggers?" He gestured at the spray of bites on Moises's ankles.

The boy scratched his legs half-heartedly. "This is my home."

"Well you are talking to the wrong man, then." He thumbed a gesture to the sleeping figure behind him. "Luis is a bore. He likes to tell me that an acre and a half of forest disappears every second and that in forty years it will all be gone. But as I say to him, so will I. Nobody wants to save me." He slapped his thighs as he laughed.

Moises sat down and took off his cap, a feeling of unreality sweeping over him again. *Was the black butterfly really out there under that tarpaulin?* He felt so alone. Maybe Geraldo would know how to get Moises out of this situation. They could split the money. He had known the man for years, but could he be trusted? Moises pulled the matchbox from his shorts and popped the gum into his mouth. Geraldo watched him intently.

"What is wrong, *Chibolo?*"

Moises chewed methodically for a few moments. "I am fine," he said and got to his feet.

After another hour on the debris-strewn Rio Marañón, Moises pulled into Prado. It was late afternoon; he still had three hours of natural light left.

The village consisted of around thirty thatched houses, one of which had been ceded to him by his employers. In the centre of the wide, grassy street was his neighbour Walter's *tienda*. Some scrawny chickens scattered half-heartedly as Moises approached the man.

"You are back," Walter observed.

"Yes." Moises lowered his bags onto the sticky mud and bought three sugar apples from the man. He raised his arms above his head and cracked his shoulders then shook his legs to loosen them up.

Walter stood up and handed him the fruit. The old man's leathery face slowly formed a quizzical smile. "Why are you back so soon?"

"I am feeling sick." Moises paid the man and trudged up

the street to his house. Two young boys were sitting on his step. On the floor beneath them, their pet Goliath beetles turned circles in the mud. The boys had tied strings around their glossy carapaces and were tugging at them without interest. As Moises approached, their hands came out automatically. He dropped two five centimo coins into them and hurried inside.

Moises took time to make a *Challa*, toasting Pachamama by spilling a little *chicha morada* upon the hut floor and then drinking the rest of the bitter-sweet drink. He opened a sugar apple and gulped down the custard-like flesh. The table was a mess of opened paint tubes and half-finished canvass boards. He picked up his Chagall book and began turning the pages slowly, studying the vivid paintings on the pages. Then, as if coming out of a trance, he dropped the book back on the table and swept everything onto the floor.

Moises closed his eyes for a moment. *Walter might be Dollie's spy.* The thought jostled with all the others in his fevered head. *It doesn't matter … I have to continue.*

He pulled on some surgical gloves and removed the insect from the net with a pair of forceps, working beneath the window that caught the evening sun. On the specially constructed spreading board, he pinned the butterfly through the thorax, inserting a light insect pin into the front part of each forewing. Then he gently teased them forward so they sat at right angles to the body. He repeated the procedure for the hind wings.

"I want to help," Moises whispered. "*Mama selva*, I want to help." He began to study the butterfly. Apart from the size, he could see only one physical difference to an ordinary butterfly; an extra pair of hook-ended antennae that hung under the sensory pair. It was one of these that had stabbed him when he injected the creature, he realised now, looking at his finger for the first time since the incident. There was a slight swelling around the small puncture.

He opened Hawthorne's book on microscopy and another on the anatomy of butterflies. He began to set up the stereo microscope as he had practised so many times in the past year, slowly regaining his composure as he worked. *Will it be powerful enough?* He would find out very soon.

Moises manoeuvred the eyepiece over the left forewing. He turned the tiny, powerful, LED light on and focused the eyepiece. There were hundreds of chitinous scales, possibly thousands: rectangular near the thorax, narrowing toward the outer edges of the wings. The overlapping rows reminded him of the rooftops in Iquitos. At 40x, Moises became aware of some discolouration on parts of the scales. He increased magnification and pulled the light a little closer, following instructions from the books at every step, skip-reading, flicking pages back and forth in exasperation: pigmentation compounds ... structural colour ... light reflection interacting with wing structure ...

*"Es imposible,"* he muttered. He didn't even understand many of the words in the book. It occurred to him that he might look forever and not happen upon the right combination of angle, light and magnification.

"I'm on your side ... *que me ayudes,"* Moises whispered over and over, as if the spirit of the butterfly could hear him. He swung the modified head of the microscope across to the outer edge of the opposite forewing and rotated the objective turret to 60x. Longitudinal and horizontal ribbing was now visible on the scales. He could see that there was something in between the lines: lighter, irregular shapes he hadn't noticed before. He upped the objective to 80x then finally 100x. Bringing his left hand across to steady his quivering right, he slowly sharpened the focus.

Moises pulled his head up, rubbed his eyes and stared out of the window for a moment. He felt uncomfortable all of a sudden, as if his senses had reached an acuteness that was painful. The fading sunlight seemed a little warmer, the jungle a little greener, the cries of the hoatzin birds vibrated much more clearly in his ears. He picked out the vanilla aroma of a planifolia orchid out there somewhere amongst the moist reek of vegetation.

The impossible was true.

He went back to the microscope and delirious with anticipation, spun the head to and fro, unable to settle for more than a moment on anything in particular. His scalp began to tingle, goose bumps ran down his back and made his buttocks twitch. He blinked again and again, as his new eyes, because new they felt, processed what was emerging from the magnified darkness of the wing. Vast landscapes of writing stretching away in all directions, overlapping the scales flawlessly, appearing at once as text and simultaneously as shivering images, which bloomed and swayed in his mind like fields of impossible flowers turning under an unpredictable breeze.

Moises pulled his sweaty hands away and ran them down his shirt, trying to calm himself. He had an instinctive feeling that what he was seeing wasn't writing at all, and this scared him more than anything else. For a moment he thought about running, but he quickly dismissed the notion and concentrated his mind on what he was seeing.

Fighting a powerful instinct to browse, Moises picked a story at random and began to read …

# OVER THE TOWN

Kirov Street was a terrifying place.

Endless lines of horseless carts coughed and roared in a deathless procession, searching the night, cutting at it with unforgiving lights. The wind came down the wide road in a freezing flood, whipping up rubbish that swirled amongst the pedestrians like large, dirty snowflakes. Overhead, in the wild darkness, electric cables sang a song that the couple could not understand. They had been in Vitebsk for an unknown period of time, following the huge, frantic highway that snaked through the city and studying the flat-roofed buildings that lined either side.

The young man, Vital, finally noticed something familiar across the road.

"There, Maria, I think we've found it," he said, pointing a gloved hand. He edged closer to the kerb. It had to be what they were searching for: three giant, arched windows, each one divided by a stone column, just as described to them by Tymokh the farmer earlier that day. They would have to cross the road to reach it.

The young woman leaned in towards her husband. "I think we'll have to fly over."

Vital shook his head. "It's not possible here. The wind will break us."

As if to confirm his prediction, Maria was lifted from the pavement by a vicious gust. Vital threw his arms around her waist and his toes left the ground for a terrifying moment as he pulled her back down. They huddled together, watching the steady stream of vehicles flash past.

"Up there, down here, what's the difference?"

Vital took his wife's hand firmly. "It will be okay, I promise. Move quickly when I tell you."

He studied the road to his left, searching for any large breaks in the approaching traffic. The traffic was heavy, but not moving slowly enough for the couple to slip across easily. Still, they could not go back. Time, the impossible new reality, was urging them forward without mercy. Vital turned to Maria and took the holdall she was carrying.

"Do you see it?"

Maria held onto the hood of her coat and concentrated on the gap in the traffic approaching them. "Don't leave me."

Vital gripped her hand, "I never will."

The lovers ran out onto the road, their delicate feet skipping like flat stones across a millpond. When they reached the central reservation, Vital stopped and shouted something that was lost in the wind. He put his arm around Maria's back and gripped the cold metal barrier with both hands, shielding her with his body. Carriages droned past on either side, almost dragging the couple back into the road. The lights, the noise, the ruptured wind; it was all too much to withstand. Vital jumped over the barrier, not because he was sure of his choice, but because he simply couldn't stay there any longer without crumbling. Maria followed his loping run and as they crossed the open car park in front of the station, the wind fell away as if finally conceding defeat.

It was still beneath the tall portico at the entrance.

"We did it," Maria panted. She looked back across the road. "They sit so still inside those carts. How do they do that?"

The station foyer was high-ceilinged and filled with a stiff, uninviting light. There were many people gathered around the walls, studying writing that the lovers could not read. In places, the red floor tiles were worn to dirty pink, forming paths that converged near the ticket counters or led to the platforms. Vital hurried Maria across.

"Destination?" the old man behind the glass asked. The lines in his face deepened as he considered the young man and the woman sheltering behind him.

Vital opened his mouth. No sound came out.

"Which service?"

Maria shivered against his back.

He concentrated. "Two for Moscow please." The words tinkled against the glass in front of him. The ticket seller shifted in his seat and tapped some keys.

"Ages?"

"Eighteen."

"Visas please."

Vital moved toward the glass. "Visas?"

"You require a visa to travel from Belarus to Russia."

"We must get to Moscow," Vital said.

"Not without visas you won't."

Vital sensed a queue forming behind them. "We are sick," he said and took his glasses off.

The old man recoiled. "*Bozha moj!* My God, is it contagious?"

"No, no, and we have money … lots of money."

The ticket collector stood up and looked around the station quickly. He rubbed his hands up and down the front of his trousers and sat down again. "Not contagious?"

Vital shook his head and thrust a bunch of crumpled notes onto the counter. The old man counted the money carefully. His face brightened a little. He pushed some of the cash into the till and the rest into his jacket pocket. He tapped some keys and told them that no changes were required on the service. A machine next to him chattered violently and spat out their tickets.

"Platform eight," he said, but they were already walking away.

They sat on plastic seats that grew from the walls like tough fungi. Vital opened the scrap of paper that the old farmer had given him before they had set off that afternoon. Tymokh had drawn a crude clock face with the hands in a particular position and a swirling shape, which signified the correct platform to be at when the clock on the wall matched the drawing. Vital looked up at the clock for the duration of one sweep of the second hand, noting how far the first hand moved in that time. They had clocks at home of course, but there was no reason for them to move. The concept of time was still indistinct. He knew enough to realise it was their enemy.

The station was busy with evening commuters. Great plumes of steam rolled from their mouths as they hurried past. Some of them glanced at the lovers as if sensing a difference about them.

"Will we make it through this strangeness?" Maria asked, nodding at the coffee shop opposite them where people sat together, raising and lowering their cups in what appeared to be a languid, passionless ritual.

"Of course we will make it," Vital replied. "The train is coming."

The couple went to the heavy doors that led to platform eight. When a man opened them, they slipped through behind him and hurried down a set of steel steps. Under the platform's creaking roof, lanterns swung a lurid light back and forth in the wind. They put their backs to the wall and waited.

There was a slight trembling in the ground as their train rolled up. The metal tube hissed and opened. Maria began to shiver as she looked into the squares of light, at the people who sat so still inside them.

"I can't!" she said.

A whistle blew. "You must!" Vital urged.

"They'll see us, it's too bright, it's not going to work."

"Trust me." He held out his hand.

Maria looked at his eyes, at the sweep of his nose and the delicate swirls around his cheekbones.

"*Ja ciabe kakhaju.*" Something spilled from her eye and splashed white on the concrete as they ran for the closing doors.

They sat in the emptiest carriage at the rear of the train. Vital laid the tickets out on the pale, smooth table. He picked up a newspaper somebody had left behind and opened it to form a shield against prying eyes. For a while he stared at the creased pages, wondering what the tiny black shapes on them might mean. When the train was moving, he lowered the paper for a moment.

"Can I eat now?" Maria asked.

Vital had a quick look around. There were only five other people in the carriage, two of whom were asleep. He nodded.

Maria picked up the holdall between her feet and lifted it onto the table. Inside it there was another bag, which shimmered with shades of pink and lilac. She pulled off her gloves quickly and for a moment her elegant hands fluttered over the provisions like mating butterflies. She took out a cobalt-blue flask, which leaned awkwardly when set on the table. Two small packages wrapped in paper followed: a flat round of rye bread and a wedge of sweet, heavy cake. Maria unscrewed the lid of the flask and filled it up with Okroshka. Vital declined her offer and her excitement fell as quickly as it had risen. She turned to face the window and sipped the cold soup. The glass rocked rhythmically, revealing the surprising strangeness of her own face.

When the ticket collector came, Vital laid the newspaper over their provisions. The man punched their tickets, flung them onto the table and moved on. When Vital picked the paper up again, the pages were dotted with yellow ochre, cobalt blue and raw umber.

"Is it really there?" Maria asked him, noticing the hairline cracks that had developed in his cheeks since they had boarded the train.

"Of course, but we have to be quick because–"

"Tomorrow it shuts forever."

"Yes."

He jumped to his feet and headed for the toilet. "I'll be back soon," he managed.

Maria stood up.

"Stay here," he said.

Heads rose along the carriage. Maria sank back into her seat as her husband stumbled out.

Vital leaned over the sink and stared into the trembling mirror. He saw himself clearly for the first time: A simple figure whose eyes swirled with questions and fear of the answers to them.

When the fog came to the village, everyone sensed its destructive power. It was thick, impenetrable and rotten smelling. It loosened the skin and burned the eyes. Most people stayed indoors in an effort to lessen its effects, but nothing could protect them. On the outskirts of the village, houses began to fall in great slaps of colour.

In desperation, Vital did something nobody had even considered before. He struck out into the dark, colourless woods that surrounded their home and came out the other side with no idea what he was searching for. For a time, he trudged along the roadside without hope. Then he noticed a newspaper flapping in a bush.

There was a picture of him and Maria on one of its pages.

Vital took the newspaper and sat by the banks of the Zapadnaya Dvina River, unwilling to go back to the village without an answer. He watched the nearby farmhouse as the sun passed across the barren sky. Eventually, he realised what he must do. When the old man came out again to feed his animals, Vital approached him.

Overcoming his initial shock, the man invited Vital into his house. He read the newspaper for Vital, looking up from the print constantly, as if unable to believe what his eyes were telling him.

After some bartering, Tymokh told Vital how he and Maria might make their way to Moscow. He supplied the clothes needed to hide the couple's strange physique and the roubles for the train fare. In return, Vital brought candlesticks, goblets and trinkets he thought would appease the man. When they left for Moscow, Vital gave Tymokh a peacock as a parting gift. The old farmer threw it among the chickens in his yard. They tore it to pieces and the mud was soaked a dazzling blue.

From these bewildering moments, others quickly followed, like a string of beads snapping, tumbling one after another until Vital found himself staring into a mirror on a train: a train rattling relentlessly through the night, heading for a place called Moscow, where the lovers would alight with no money and no way of returning home.

Removing a glove, Vital held his hand up and studied it in the spotlight above the sink. With careful deliberation, he ran his finger across the mirror, spelling out the name that was in the newspaper he had found, the name Tymokh had taught him.

## CHAGALL

The letters were running down the glass as he left the toilet.

The train arrived in Moscow just before six in the morning and the couple slipped off like ghosts. The first road they found was eight lanes across, but the traffic was light. They hurried across, gripped by a sudden elation. They had survived the road, the terrible wind and the train. Now, impossibly, they were within reach of their destination. Vital felt something change in him. The fear he had been holding since they left the village, left his body quite suddenly as they crossed. He pulled on Maria's arm, grinning at her, and whooping at the lightening sky in a sudden, exuberant release of nervous tension.

He forgot about the kerb at the other side, saw it at the last moment and lifted his feet in panic, imagining them snapping against the hard step of concrete. It was too late. Vital put his right arm out to break his fall and tried to roll into it.

Maria went to him. "Darling, are you all right?"

Vital got up slowly and shook his right arm. A thick flurry of flakes fell to the ground. He felt no pain, none physical anyway, just a deep sense of loss at the strange looseness in the arm of his coat.

"Help me take my glove off … carefully." He held his left arm out. Maria gently pulled the glove off. His index finger and thumb were gone. She shook the glove. The two digits fell to the pavement, softened and broke apart, then ran into the cracks.

"What is happening to you?" she asked.

He looked into her eyes. "We have to be quick."

After that they took the subways that ran under the huge roads. Grizzled men huddled at the entrances, arguing to the beat of painful music, their cigarettes blazing and fading like fireflies succumbing to the cold. Inside, *babushki* sat behind tiny, haphazard stalls littered with guttering candles. The old women held out jars of pickled vegetables and pairs of tights as the couple hurried past.

The sun was hidden behind formless clouds when they reached the State Tretyakov Gallery. The building was white and low, its glass facade shimmering with cold light. The couple approached it. They stood in front of the locked doors for some time.

"What now?" Maria asked.

"The old man may have lied to us."

The wind came down from above with a fine drizzle, catching at the corner of the laminated poster on the doors. It was an artist's impression of a gleaming steel and glass building, similar to the one in front of them but much taller. There were people drawn in the foreground, walking past a fountain or sitting under ornamental trees.

"Why?"

"I'm not sure."

"But the paper said–"

"Tymokh said," Vital snapped. "We don't know what the paper really had on its pages. Maybe it's not here now … or it never was." He stopped himself abruptly, feeling ashamed. He wanted to go home.

"Can we go back?"

Vital shook his head.

There was movement from within the gallery. A short, fat, middle-aged woman was making her way towards the front doors. Her feet were splayed and the left leg bowed outwards below the knee, causing her to rise and fall as she walked. A set of large keys hung from her hand. She opened the tall, glass doors and appraised the couple.

"Your hoods, take them down."

They obliged.

"Let me see … You have come from Vitebsk?"

"Yes. How do you know?"

"Chagall came from there." She ushered them in. They passed through another set of doors and entered a reception area. A young man in an ill-fitting uniform sat behind a desk. The woman flicked her head as she passed him. "We've got another two."

The man grunted.

They passed through long corridors bathed in bright light. Vital and Maria followed the woman in silence, listening to her uneven gait play its strange rhythm on the polished, wooden floor. Occasionally, one of them noticed something wondrous in one of the many rooms they passed and stopped. She came back to them every time, grunting with effort.

"That's a Pavel Filinov," she would say. "This one's a Serov … a Kandinsky … ah yes, Goncharova – 'Peacock in the Bright Sunlight'. Beautiful isn't it? Come along now, I don't want you making a mess in here on my last day."

Finally, the woman stopped and turned into one of the rooms. For the first time, she looked at their faces.

"This is what you came for, isn't it?" she asked, moving aside.

The lovers gasped and stepped forward.

"Don't touch," she said quickly. "There are still some rich people who want this sort of thing."

Maria studied the painting. "It's us … and the village. It's really us, perhaps–"

"It's called 'Over the Town'," the woman continued. "And no, it can't help you. It's just a painting."

Vital held out his broken hand to the curator. "I don't understand."

The woman sighed. "I've worked in this museum for thirty years. I remember when people used to flock here. I don't know, maybe they put their dreams into these paintings when they looked at them. Maybe their love brought you to life … kept you alive."

She shrugged and picked at a large mole on her cheek.

"They love other things now."

Vital stepped closer to the painting. He could see their house. He wondered if it was still standing. A dizzying feeling swept through him and Maria's arm went around his waist, just as he was about to fall. The colours in the painting began to loosen and bleed slowly into the room until Vital almost believed he was home again.

"You can't stay here," the old woman said.

The rain was light and cool outside. They sat on a bench which faced the road and lowered their hoods again. The street was filling up with people.

"Was Chagall one of these?" Maria asked.

"Yes, I think he was."

"They don't look like gods."

The young man kissed his lover on the cheek and they ran together for a moment. "I don't think they know they are," he said. "Do you remember our date? How tightly I held your hand, so scared you might fly away." He took her hand as if to remind her, and looked in wonder as it melted into his, like paint on a palette.

Maria smiled, but it slipped a little. "Yes, you wouldn't come up."

"You looked so beautiful above me in that dress, floating in its purple waves."

"Will you fly away with me now?" she asked.

"Soon, *Ja ciabe kakhaju.*"

"I love you, too."

Vital and Maria sat on the bench and watched the people hurrying past each other. Some of them talked into small boxes held to their cheeks, others had things pushed into their ears that made their lips move noiselessly. They hardly glanced at the odd-looking couple who smiled contentedly, as they remembered a world without perspective, filled with music and colour and flying cows.

The man stopped at the side of the road and sighed. He pinched the roll-up against his lips and had one last, long suck before flicking it away. He stamped the stub out, picked it up with his litter-picker and deposited it in the trolley. He took a swig of aftershave and reluctantly went over to the bench to sort through the clothes lying on it. The man didn't notice the pool of multi-coloured paint beneath the bench until he felt it pulling at his boots. He looked down in disgust at the two pairs of shoes and mumbled an obscenity. *It must be the latest craze*, he thought, vaguely remembering seeing other such vandalisms in the area. When he turned, there was a short, ugly woman standing just a few feet away. She was watching him. She had a strange look on her face.

"Dumb kids," he said, gesturing at the dripping coat in his hand.

The woman turned away. He laughed at her funny walk as she made her way back towards the museum.

★ ★ ★

…Moises pulled back from the microscope and stretched his arms. Outside the hut, he could hear a mother calling her children in for supper. It was getting dark. Sheets of yellowing paper were pinned on the hut wall above his desk. One of them had the name and address of Hawthorne's parents on it. Moises had made a promise to contact them if anything happened to their son. Something *had* happened, but what could he tell Margaret and Colin Hawthorne of 16, Derwent Avenue, Luton?

The address had an exotic taste to Moises's mind. He wondered what it looked like. And wondering, went back to the butterfly and began to read …

# THEY SANG
# BEFORE MEMORY

The stick just didn't belong there. That was Margaret Hawthorne's first thought upon seeing it and the feeling wouldn't go away. She slammed the shovel down into the compacted clay soil and knelt, wincing at the dry crack of her knees. *Why did you jump, you old fool?* She wondered. *It's just a stick.* But it wasn't just a stick; Margaret knew that instinctively, just as she knew it wasn't a piece of junk, or a bone, or a piece of antiquity that she might have recognised in some vague fashion. It was unlike anything she had ever seen before. Around 20 inches long and resembling a curved piece of polished wood, it shimmered like nacre in the cool morning light, revealing an organic quality. Its vibrancy was a little unnerving.

Margaret picked it up cautiously between thumb and forefinger. She could see a system of many small holes on one side of the object. She took her gardening gloves off. Her intuition had been correct. The stick was warm.

She turned it over and over, mumbling a discussion as to the possible age and purpose of the piece. She looked around her at the broken earth, at the trays of marigolds and lobelia that she had bought from B&Q the previous evening. Had she dug this spot before? No, she was digging where the old water feature had sat: a reconstituted stone well with a bucket suspended above, which filled to tipping point with fizzing water, emptied with a whoosh and swung back to fill again. She had always found the repetitions relaxing. The well had been there twenty years ago when Margaret and Colin moved in, and she had finally agreed that it should go to the tip the previous October.

She liked the feel of the stick in her hands, the comforting warmth. The holes ran in a random pattern. It was not hollow and there was no mouthpiece; her fingers moved over the tiny holes, trying different combinations in an effort to unlock the object's purpose. Margaret realised that sometimes, when her fingers were in a certain position, she felt a slight suction from some of the holes. It was like having a tiny vacuum cleaner placed against the tip of each finger. She began to work methodically. When she felt a tug, she kept that finger in position and re-arranged the others. When seven of her fingers could feel the suction, something happened. A small shock like static electricity pulsed through her hands and she heard a melody so fragile, so compassionate, that water sprang to her eyes like blood to a fresh cut.

Margaret let out a small, shrill cry and shook away the stick. The singing stopped.

She looked at her hands, as if searching for something to help orientate herself again. It didn't help. She stayed quite still for a minute or so, listening to the regular thrum of passing traffic and occasionally turning her head to watch the blue tits going back and forth to the bird box on the garage wall. At this time of year, Margaret liked to put her ear up to the box and listen to the delicate cries of the chicks.

Finally, she forced herself to look down at the stick. It lay in the mud where she'd tossed it, like a rare conch flung up from the seabed by a violent storm. Margaret stifled a sob and reached out. Her fingers seemed to remember which holes to cover instinctively.

The sound of children.

Margaret heard them laughing and taunting each other, rattling sticks along the fence as they passed the back garden. Something about the familiar noises unsettled her. She looked around the garden dreamily, noting the spade upright in the mud, the flowers still in their plastic trays. Her hands felt numb with cold. She looked down at them and it came to her like a slap in the face. The children were coming home from the secondary school across the main road. She had lost three hours.

She ran to the house and once inside, placed the stick upon the windowsill, her eyes returning to it again and again as she drifted back and forth across the linoleum, like an automaton programmed in the basics of domestication. She found herself opening cupboards and drawers, finding ingredients, measuring them, mixing them. She washed and diced and gauged cooking times, her mind utterly focused on the job at hand and yet somehow removed from it all.

When the table was set and the pots bubbling gently, Margaret went into the lounge and sat on the sofa. Her head still felt thick, as if she had taken a couple of glasses of wine at lunchtime. She was angry with herself, wasting a day's holiday that she had set aside for gardening, just daydreaming it away like that. She turned on the television. A cheap American soap opera: a man argued with another man about the first man's wife who had lost her memory in a car crash and was being brainwashed by the second man who ... Margaret pressed the remote: a slack-jawed young man on a stage and two young women screaming obscenities at each other while two burly men held them apart ... She pressed again: two men in harnesses were swinging through the air, trying to stick coloured balls onto a giant target; below them, a large crowd screamed encouragement.

Margaret ran to the toilet, but was sick before she got there. Colin listened to her patiently, his face smooth as Margaret recounted what had happened earlier. Arriving home, he had found pans boiled dry on the stove and a cut of beef reduced to clinker in the oven. His normally composed wife was in a state close to apoplexy. He stopped her over and over again to question or check something, not believing half of the story, but anxious to diffuse her anguish. When he felt he had calmed Margaret as much as he was going to, Colin picked up the stick as she had been repeatedly asking him to do. It took a couple of minutes to get his fingers on the correct holes. Afterwards, brushing the tears from his eyes, he called the police.

Two officers came to the house and listened to the stick. They were upset, bewildered; they called it in. Their superiors, following a set procedure they didn't understand, made a number of calls and eventually, the Head of the Metropolitan Police was informed. He knew only to ring somebody unnamed in the upper echelons of the Government. That somebody knew somebody else, who understood what had occurred. His name was Mr Bank. Within two hours, he was sitting in Colin and Margaret's lounge, drinking tea.

"It's very rare to find these relics nowadays, especially in the developed world." He was a tall man with big hands and a huge froth of greying beard. "But, of course, occasionally …" He gestured at the artefact that lay on the coffee table between him and the Hawthornes.

In the doorway to the kitchen, two plain-clothed officers shuffled about like unwanted guests at a party. Everyone kept glancing back at the stick, as if expecting it to speak or move or do something even more incredible.

Margaret began to speak and Colin raised a hand.

"So you're expecting us to believe that this thing … what it sings about … that it's all–"

"All true I'm afraid. It's quite a shock, I know."

"Rubbish! I'm sorry but this won't do." Colin's face

darkened as he leaned forward. There were so many arguments against what he was being told. He simply didn't know where to begin. "Ten thousand years ago?"

"Yes, give or take."

"But carbon dating disproves that in a second."

"Yes, of course it does, Mr Hawthorne, as could a number of other scientific procedures."

Colin turned to his wife triumphantly. "You see! Utter nonsense!"

"I'm afraid not. We as a species find and create proof all the time. Subconsciously, we make science fit. And if it doesn't fit, we overlook it."

"Overlook it? Somebody would realise."

"Only when something like this happens."

"So why doesn't it get out?" Margaret asked.

"People forget."

"Forget?" Colin gestured at the stick. "How can anyone forget something like that?"

They all studied it for a moment.

"I'll come to that presently."

"It's all nonsense."

"I realise it must sound that way to you. Look, occasionally we find a suitable planet, like this one. We set things up, put a population in place and move on. People then do what comes naturally. Cultural and genetic memories fill in the spaces."

"What do you mean, 'set things up'?"

"Among other things, we suffer from nostalgia. So we go back to a point in our history and try it all again without memory, to see if we can get it right. Little changes, however ... well ... it seems we are fated to repeat the same mistakes." Mr Bank leaned back in his chair and sipped his tea. He didn't look crazy at all. "You see, this planet will eventually wear out like all the others.

It's difficult to hold back human progress." He smiled as if to apologise.

"My God!" Margaret whispered. "So where are we now, I mean in terms of this planet's sustainability?" She laughed at her own question. It was all so ridiculous, like an absurd play they were practising, each one of them with their own outrageous lines to recite.

Mr Bank brightened a little. "We are doing pretty well: on the cusp of a downward trend. This is about as good as it gets."

"Let me get this straight. This is not Earth?" Colin asked, snorting incredulously.

"No it isn't. The original Earth was quite a bit different to this one, so I'm led to believe. Luckily, by the time we'd broken it, there was the technology to move on."

The Hawthornes, a double act perfecting incredulity, stared at Mr Bank for a few moments. It was Margaret's turn.

"And we just repeat it all? How many times?"

"I'm not sure to be honest: many, many times."

"Oh God!"

Mr Bank gave Margaret a sour look for a second, as if her words, so full of disgust, were wounding him. He took a digestive from his saucer and bit off a tiny piece, chewing it slowly. "I'm sorry this has happened to you, but–"

"It appears we don't integrate very well," Colin remarked to his wife.

Mr Bank scratched behind his right ear. His face seemed to settle a little, the show of joviality drained from the lines around his eyes. He set his teacup back onto the occasional table beside him with a clink.

"It's inevitable that there are casualties to indigenous species, I'm afraid."

"Casualties? It's called genocide."

"Our nature is to conquer."

"It's an outrage!" Margaret stated. She looked at Colin for something as she always did when distressed. For the first time in their twenty-five year marriage, he came up short. His mouth worked silently, as if trying to vocalise something profound, but nothing came out. He took Margaret's hand and they sat in silence on the edge of the sofa. Mr Bank studied them both.

"These painful memories will leave you," he said gently, "a genetic trick we seem to have developed."

"I don't want to forget."

"I know Mrs Hawthorne, but it's for the best. I, and a few chosen others, will remember it for you."

For a moment Mr Bank caught Margaret's eyes and she saw the weariness there and had to look away. He rose and wiped his mouth.

"Thanks for the tea."

"I want–"

"Can't let you have it, I'm afraid." He picked the stick up from the coffee table and walked briskly from the room with his escorts. Then the front door clicked shut, leaving them in silence.

That night, Margaret dreamed of a grey child with wide, dark eyes.

*His world was sap green and ocean blue. He rose and fell through the sky with his siblings, emitting strangely empathic sounds. Margaret could see the songs like watercolours spreading against the clouds above.*

*Suddenly, the air split as bright, deafening shapes ripped through it and bruised the planet's surface. There came a flood of pale, clumsy things that jabbered painfully and dashed here and there.*

*On the day he was to be taken along with his family to the factories, the grey child sang a diary and thrust it into the earth, as filthy brown smoke belched into the sky on the horizon.*

Margaret awoke with a gasp. She sighed and eased back onto her pillow, breathing deeply as she studied the swirls of Artex on the ceiling. She was clammy from a recurring dream that she could never quite remember. The digital clock by her bed said 10.17 a.m.

Downstairs, she stood at the sink for a while, sipping a coffee, hugging the mug as she gazed out of the rain-slashed window at her back garden. The men from the Government had dug it all up and then re-landscaped it as she had always wanted. Apparently, a WW2 bomb had been found nearby and to make sure there were no more around, they had dug the whole street up. No expense had been spared and yet the garden gave her little pleasure anymore. She didn't seem to have the energy for it, or the enthusiasm.

Margaret realised the coffee was cool in her hands and flicked the kettle back on. She sat in the living room for a while, staring at the mantelpiece, watching the second hand on the carriage clock make its incremental climb and fall, following a well-worn pattern of inertia that had gripped her since the bomb had been found. What had come over her? She was so scared all the time and she was … well, sad – infinitely and crushingly sad, and she didn't have the faintest idea why. And yet there was something, something she couldn't quite get a fix on that was skirting her consciousness like a shark circling her as she trod water in the darkness. She had given up her job, her independence and was just waiting for the teeth to finish her. Whose teeth?

She decided to clean the under-stairs cupboard. At the back, between a Scrabble box and an old sewing tin, she found a shoebox with a piece of A4 taped to the side. It said, *READ ME!* The papers inside were in her handwriting. The top sheet had one line:

*Last read on October 21st 2008 – Maggie Hawthorne.*

That was last week: impossible. She went to the sheet underneath.

*Firstly, your breakdown was not caused by a late menopause*
*and there was no bomb scare. You found something …*
The words ran into the darkness behind her eyes.

When Colin came home from work she was standing by the barbecue with a large sheaf of papers in one hand and a box of matches in the other.

"Are you okay, love?"

"No, I think I've lost my mind. I found these papers, five sets of them, hidden around the house."

He put down his bag and read the papers, holding her hand gently. "You're right, Maggie, I think it's for the best."

She turned to him, her eyes like clear, glistening stones, too large for their settings. "Is it?"

He took the papers from her and put them on the grill. Margaret watched them curl and wither and as the heart of them took hold, a gush of smoke went up into the grey sky. She wanted to inhale all that smoke, all that terrible knowledge, and keep it within her, so she could look upon it sometimes and try to make sense. But it drifted away like whispers on the wind.

Margaret sat down on the sofa and tried to picture the Home Office man who had apparently come to see them: Mr Bank, wasn't it? She laughed out loud. Colin came through chewing the last of his sandwich, the *Daily Mail* in his hand.

"What's funny, love?" he asked.

"Oh nothing really. Is there anything interesting in there today?"

He looked at the paper a little sheepishly. "They've made a new find in Egypt: an emperor's tomb. It dates back almost four thousand years, they say."

"Who do?"

"Well … Egyptologists. It's a change from hearing about that bloody black butterfly anyway. They still haven't found the boy you know, after that fiasco in New York."

"Well, I'm a believer … in the butterfly I mean. It makes you think that anything is possible."

Colin turned to the sports pages and grunted. "It's all a big con. Stories only he can read that disappear after he's read them … How convenient."

She flicked on the television when Colin had gone back to work. *This Morning* was just finishing. A pet clairvoyant was telling the owner of two shih tzus that they weren't happy with the new suits she had bought for them or the new food she had introduced to their monographed bowls. They were, she said, very stressed and needed a pampering weekend at a Canine Health Spa. Phillip Schofield looked nonplussed and the lady owner looked mortified at how she had let her babies down. She promised to do something about the trauma she had caused and was close to tears as the camera pulled away from her.

Margaret turned the television off. She cried for an hour without knowing why and then went to prepare dinner. As she fumbled around at the back of the freezer, searching for a bag of chicken breasts, her hand came up against something hard and flat underneath them. She pulled the mysterious item out and stared at it for a moment. It was some ice-furred papers. Margaret brushed some of the ice crystals off and saw her own handwriting, and her heart fluttered. She had the strangest feeling, a mixture of *déjà vu* and black fear, and almost put the papers back into the freezer, but curiosity and a growing feeling of excitement changed her mind. She closed the freezer door, placed the brittle sheaf on the breadboard and waited for it to defrost.

# THE PIECRUST
# PROMISE

Adam stepped into the meadow and closed the door behind him. He held his hand over his eyes for a few moments as they adjusted to the sunshine and began walking through the pasture, relishing how the long grass licked cool and sharp at his shins. Above him, swallows criss-crossed the cloudless blue. He rolled his shoulders as he moved, sighing with contentment; it was so good to feel the sun on his back again. A dense wood lay half a mile ahead of him, still seeping mist like some primordial landscape. He increased his pace.

A young woman was sitting at the edge of the treeline on a crude bench. She had her back to Adam and did not notice him as he approached. She was wearing a white, lace-trimmed dress with a red cummerbund and a white, wide-brimmed hat. A patch of dry dirt in front of the bench was holding her attention and her feet, clad in white, leather sandals, kept darting out to stamp at it. She stood with a growl of exasperation and began jumping up and down, throwing her arms around and grunting with emphasis every time her feet hit the ground. It was a petulant, childish act and Adam found it incredibly attractive.

"There!" she said triumphantly, delivering one final stamp.

"You look beeyootiful, Mary Poppins," Adam declared.

The woman gave a startled yelp and spun around to face him. Her hand skipped to her chest. "Oh my God! Don't do that! I nearly had a heart attack."

Adam put down the picnic hamper. "Sorry," he laughed. "You jumped a mile."

"It's not funny! Feel my heart." She grabbed his hand and went to put it to her chest, but thought better of it and let it go again. "Never mind."

Adam looked down at her feet. "What were you doing anyway?"

The woman sighed and readjusted her lace hat. "Killing ants … Killing time really."

"Are you going to a fancy dress party or something?"

"No, I always dress this way." She gave him a sharp look and sat on the bench with a sigh, smoothing her dress underneath her. "I'm going to fry in this thing."

Adam sat next to her, quite close, and she didn't shuffle away. "That's my favourite film," he said, pointing at her dress.

"It is? Mine, too."

"A bit early to be going to a party, isn't it?"

"Ha, well, I was going to meet my boyfriend, have a few drinks first and make a day of it, you know?"

"Sounds a good plan."

She got to her feet again. "But the thing is, he's a …" Her face clouded over for a moment. "… *pinga*. I mean dickhead. Is that right?"

"Er, I'm not sure."

"Doesn't matter." She shook her head and smiled. "What the hell's up with me? Anyway, I don't really want to be with him today." She rattled on for a couple of minutes then, telling Adam that this Phil had once cheated on her with her best friend, Chloe, how he never took her anywhere and how he always humiliated her in front of his friends. It all came out of her in a torrent of expletives and rhetorical questions and then abruptly dried up.

They sat in silence for a few seconds.

"So … are you going to the party or not?" Adam asked.

The two of them burst into laughter. The woman undid the ribbon tied under her chin and whisked her hat into the sky. It hung in the flawless blue for a moment, before falling into the trees ahead of them.

"Oh bugger! I better get that or I'll lose my deposit." She hitched her dress a little and trotted towards the wood. Adam picked up her parasol and followed her into the cool silence beneath the trees. Narrow corridors of bluebells and pink purslane lay before him between smooth, soaring columns of beech. Countless butterflies bobbed and winked in the cathedral stillness.

"Beautiful isn't it?" the woman said quietly as he joined her.

"Beautiful," he agreed and held out his hand. "I'm Adam."

"I'm Gabriella." They shook hands with an awkward formality.

"Well," he said, "I'm going for a picnic. Want to come?"

"You picnic alone?"

"I will be, unless you join me."

"That's pretty weird, going for a picnic alone. Do you have champagne?"

"Of course. Never go anywhere without it."

"In that case, I'll take the chance. Surely psychopaths don't carry champagne. I'd better take that, it doesn't suit you." Gabriella took the parasol from Adam and set off into the wood, moving unhurriedly, as though the wood were familiar to her. He gradually fell further behind, content to watch her drifting through the trees like a lost, Edwardian ghost.

Eventually she stopped and waited for him. "You are slow," she said as he caught her up.

"Be nice! I've got the provisions remember? Plus, there is still a chance I'm a psychopath."

"Good point."

Adam became aware of the sound of running water coming from the trees to his right. He stepped off the track, pushed through a thick tangle of low-hanging branches and came out on the other side, his face peppered with tiny welts of blood. To his right was a clear, gurgling stream, filled with long, wavy strands of harlequin-green weed. The water came down a tumble of smooth pebbles and swirled into a small pond right in front of him. He fell to his knees.

"Gabriella, look at this."

She appeared from his left, having taken a more circuitous but clearer route, and knelt down beside him. He was slurping at a palmful of water.

Gabriella cupped her hands and brought some water to her lips. "What have you done? You're bleeding," she said and took out a handkerchief.

"I'm fine," he protested, but allowed her to wet the cloth in the pool and carefully wipe his face.

There was a little love seat beside the brook, carved out of oak. They clasped hands without thinking and sat for a while, lulled into a quiet reverence. Mayflies were hovering over the pond, tempting the silent predators beneath the surface.

"They are of the order Ephemeroptera," Adam said after a time.

Gabriella opened one eye, smiling. "What?"

He pointed. "From the Greek *Ephemeros*, meaning 'short-lived wing'."

"What are you talking about?"

"The mayflies; they only live for between a half hour and one day … depending on the species that is."

She stared at him. "One day? That is so sad."

"I suppose it is." He pointed at the water. "Look! Brown trout I think."

"Oh yes," said Gabriella, noticing the sleek shapes suspended in crystal. "How do you know all this stuff?"

"You need to in my occupation."

She stood up and dusted herself down. "Which is?"

"I'm a biological engineer."

Gabriella pulled a face. "Oh I see. So I should be impressed?"

He grinned. "I would be."

"Do you live nearby then?" Gabriella asked.

"No, never been here before. Just visiting. And you?"

She opened her mouth to speak and then paused. Adam saw something move in her eyes, confusion perhaps, like fish startled in muddy water.

"*Vengo* ... er, I come here often."

They went back to the track and walked into the heart of the wood. Adam pointed out a red squirrel clinging to a high branch, explaining to Gabriella the rarity of the species. They sang 'Supercalifragilisticexpialidocious' and 'Chim Chim Cheree', and didn't meet one other person all morning.

They came to a clearing with a giant oak tree standing in it. Clumps of daffodils had sprung up in the splashes of sunlight. Gabriella came up behind Adam and wrapped her arms around his waist. He felt her breasts spreading against his back.

"This is nice," she breathed into his ear.

He shivered and his stomach tensed. "Yes it is."

Adam opened the hamper and laid out a red chequered blanket in a pool of sunshine. Gabriella kicked off her shoes as she stepped onto it. "Undo me."

His hands were shaking as they unzipped her dress, as if this were the unveiling of a sculpture he had commissioned someone to carve and he was embarrassed by how much he had paid for it. The dress fell and Gabriella was naked underneath. She let her hair down and turned to Adam, and before he could think of something clever to say, she was undoing his shorts. He kicked off his shoes and threw away his tee shirt as they fell onto the blanket in a clumsy frenzy.

It was over very quickly and they parted without meeting each other's eyes, rolling away like children giving up at playing mums and dads, embarrassed at how much they had revealed of themselves and how little it added up to. For a couple of minutes Adam lay on his back, unable to move, feeling prickly waves of embarrassment roll through him.

Gabriella crawled over on her elbows and kissed his cheek. "Do you want to have another go?"

He did.

Afterwards, she fell asleep in the crook of his arm and he followed her, soothed by the hammering of a green woodpecker and the soughing of the wind through the treetops.

When he woke, she was already sitting up. "You snore, Bucko," she said.

"What? No way!"

"Do so!" She offered him a bottle of water.

He took a sip, watching the swing of her breasts as she plated some food for him.

"Will you marry me?" he asked, stunned at his own words.

"Er … yes, probably," Gabriella replied.

They both began to laugh, as if unsure if this were reality or a play they were practising.

Gabriella picked a dripping bottle of champagne from the basket, loosened the wire cage at its neck and thumbed the cork. It looped into the treetops with a hollow pop.

"I can't believe how forward I was earlier." She shook her head in disgust as she poured.

"You did take me by surprise."

"Do you think I'm easy?"

"No, of course not … Well, a bit."

She kicked him, spilling a little champagne on the blanket. "You bastard! I thought you were the *one*, too."

"Did you?"

"Well, maybe." She looked at him coyly. "I was just thinking, wouldn't it be fantastic if we brought our children here one day and told them all about how we first met? Not how easy I was, though, of course."

"No, we couldn't tell them that. It would scar them possibly … probably."

"We will have a girl and a boy: Jane and Michael." She cut him a slice of apple pie and handed it to him.

He popped a forkful into his mouth. The filling was sweet and mushy and slightly odd tasting. "Why Jane and Michael?"

"Jane and Michael from Mary Poppins?"

"Oh, of course."

"It's not your favourite film, is it? You just fancy Mary Poppins."

Adam put his plate down and raised his hands in surrender. "Okay, you got me!"

Gabriella shuffled closer. Adam shivered when her shoulder hit his and watched his goose bumps spread onto her skin. How quickly they had fallen into this easy intimacy. It disturbed him for some reason. It was exhilarating, but there was something underscoring the frivolity, something he hadn't bargained for. He felt angry about this elusive irritation and was angry about feeling angry.

"I fell for you the moment I looked up from those damned ants earlier," Gabriella said. Her voice sounded weary.

"Same here. Weird isn't it."

She rested her head upon his shoulder. "There will be more than just today wont there?"

"I promise."

Her arms clung tighter around him. "That's a piecrust promise: easily made, easily broken," she said.

Adam turned and began nuzzling her neck, feeling aroused again by her vulnerability. He found her mouth and pushed her to the ground.

The blanket was in shadow when Gabriella slipped her dress back on.

"Is it time to go *already*?"

"Yes, baby."

"Let's stay a bit longer," he tried.

She turned away from him and reluctantly, he zipped up her dress.

"We'll have to make a move. My mum will be wondering where I am. I bet Phil has rung to tell her I didn't turn up today."

When they came out of the trees, it was to a meadow which mirrored the one Adam had strolled across that morning. The sun, which had been so strong back then, was now just a warm kiss on their cheeks. A line of trees was silhouetted against the tangerine glow at the horizon, like a strip of intricately cut, black card laid over a wash of paint.

They came to a high, perfectly trimmed hedge with a door handle sticking from it. Gabriella went to open it and Adam grabbed her arm.

"Don't you want to get out of here with me?"

A look of utter confusion came over Gabriella's face. "I … no, *por favor, no se puede!*"

"Come on! Quickly!" He grabbed her hand and tried to drag her back towards the wood. But from somewhere nearby there came a hissing sound, short and sharp, and Adam felt a small prick of pain in his thigh. His legs buckled immediately, as if the bones had been snatched from them. He tore weakly at the cold grass, wondering how it had all gone so wrong.

"I'll come back, I promise."

Gabriella's startled face appeared above him, blocking out the night sky. Her lips moved soundlessly into darkness.

The young man who entered the room was hairless and brusque. His grey shell suit whispered as he sat down. He began tapping at the console in his hand and gave a narrow smile.

"Okay, Adam, all the prelims are done. I will now just confirm the details of the Lovelyday™ you have purchased. You have chosen the LateMay bracket." The man stopped tapping and looked up. "Please confirm vocally."

"Oh, sorry. I mean yes."

"You have chosen Newforest Biome."

"Yes."

"You have chosen Gabriella, with the Mary Poppins scenario you came up with yourself."

"Er ... yes."

"You're unsure?"

"No, no, it's fine. Where is she from?"

"She's Peruvian. Why?"

"No reason. Just curious."

Don't worry about the language and dialect. We will give her one to match yours; she doesn't speak good English as it stands."

Adam shrugged. "Of course, she doesn't look like Mary Poppins either but she is so pretty."

The man ignored the observation. "Your Lovelyday™ lasts for approximately ten hours, commencing at ten a.m. Biome time, three a.m. Lunar, and finishes at eight p.m. Biome time, one p.m. Lunar. You have thoroughly acquainted yourself with the rules of your engagement once inside the Biome?"

"I have."

"As previously explained, if there is any transgression at any time, your Lovelyday™ will be terminated and you will be removed from the Biome immediately. The company is licensed to use extreme force against customers if they are seen to be using unprovoked or unnecessary violence against any employee of Lovelyday™ Inc. You have seen examples in digital format of what is and isn't permissible?"

Adam winced at the memory. "Yes I have."

"Are there any questions?"

"Will Gabriella be aware of who I am at all?"

"No. The magic of first love would be marred somewhat."

Adam couldn't tell if he was being sarcastic or not.

The Lovelyday™ agent placed his hand console on the grey desk and cracked his knuckles. It was as if he had been given one genuine smile at birth and had had to make it last a lifetime; he shaved off another sliver and offered it to Adam.

"We use a process called mental delineation. We sketched your requirements, as close as we could manage, into Gabriella's mind. Today, you are exactly what she wants, so it's real love she produces."

Adam was feeling a little hot. He unbuttoned his collar. "And tomorrow she will fall in love with someone else?"

"That's right. Her memories of the day are wiped each Biome evening. She is unaware of the Biome or why she is really here until her contract is up for renewal. To her, life is the meadow, the wood and all that happens there. All the girls and boys who work in the Biomes sign up for this when they come to us."

"Sure," Adam said, but he felt unsure and it must have shown on his face.

"You're a long way from home," the man said with surprising gentleness.

"Yes, it's a strange feeling sometimes."

"That's why we are here. Our Biomes are little pieces of earth. They keep people like you sane and happy while you are here, so RKK get their Helium Three and earth gets some much-needed energy." He stood up and offered Adam his hand. "You'll have a Lovelyday™ with Gabriella. I know first-hand." He winked and Adam grinned, drawn into the show of machismo.

"I hope you're right. It's taken me a month to save for this, even with my staff discount."

The man looked unmoved. "Have a Lovelyday™, Adam."

"I'll try. One more thing," Adam said as he was leaving.

"Yes?"

"That mental delineation process you mentioned?"

"Uh huh."

"Do they use it on you as well?"

"Very good, Adam. I like it," but he had already put the smile away.


The old man placed his hands against the cold metal and pushed. The door shifted fractionally. He stepped back. Across the hall, the sound of cheap air filters throbbed from behind cracked, dented doors identical to the one in front of him. Wails of torment echoed along the long, dim corridors, fluctuating in pitch and volume so much that it was impossible for him to pinpoint their source. He took an unwanted breath of damp wall linings and dried urine, and then nodded to the man he had paid to accompany him that day. "Tom, give me a hand here."

The big man moved away from the wall where he had been resting his broad back and put his shoulder onto the door with some force. It pinged open and clapped against the internal wall. He caught it as it came back and ushered the old man in.

The room was in darkness, save for a small fire which flickered against the metal floor. The woman was huddled up next to it like a tumble of kindling that refused to burn. The old man crouched down beside her and stroked her head, waving forward his minder who flicked on a hand light. Tom trained the light on the woman's sunken features as the old man studied her. His voice shook with emotion. "Gabriella, it's me, Adam. I found you … I found you." He stepped back and his companion gently picked the woman up and put her over his shoulder.

Two rat-faced men confronted them at the entrance to the apartment run.

"Hey! Who you got there?" The first one said and pulled out a rusty knife. "You can't take our ladies. We need–"

Tom shifted the woman a little on his shoulder and his free hand brought the blunt nozzle of a gum gun into the talking man's face. The smell of heated plasteen filled the air and the man fell to the ground without a sound. His partner ducked past them and disappeared into the corridors of the main complex.

"I'll get her hooked up," the big man said and carried the woman out.

Adam watched the man on the floor scrabbling at his sealed face in a futile attempt to make an airway. He waited until the man's feet had stopped drumming and spat on him as he left the building.

Tom was putting the woman in an emergency gurney and playing with the settings.

"How is she?"

"Severely malnourished and has wet beriberi by the looks of it. Put it this way, I wouldn't take her dancing tonight." Tom pushed her into the back of the vehicle and they set off.

The two men sat in silence as they drove through the long, sterile corridors. Occasionally, they passed the homeless, who huddled around tiny paraffin cubes and pleaded for help as the car cruised slowly past. Beside them, through long windows, Adam could see the silver ash of the moon's surface, piled into ugly heaps by reckless developers. Around the seals in the glass, there were cracks here and there, growing unnoticed by those they threatened most.

"How long do you think these windows will last, Tom?"

The driver took one hand from the wheel and scratched

at his temple. "Don't reckon it matters to these poor bastards. They'll still be here when the day comes."

"It's a mess."

"We always make a mess, given the chance."

The old man nodded. After a while, he said, "I helped build the Biomes."

"That so? Must've been, what ... twenty years ago?"

"Twenty-three."

Tom raised his eyebrows. "They're ruins now."

"Once they realised it was possible to configure a mind to fall in love ... well, there's a bigger market on earth."

"Lovelyday™ Incorporated," Tom announced, in the style of the ad. "The company that retired Cupid." He slapped the steering wheel, impressed with his impersonation, then flicked his head toward the rear of the vehicle. "So who is she? An employee?"

"Yes. I became a bit obsessed. They terminated my contract and sent me home."

"And you decide to come back now, when everyone who can is leaving?"

"My aunt died last year, left me some money. For once, I didn't put it in my veins ... not all of it anyway."

Tom made no comment.

"I always was awkward," Adam added.

"Awkward and stupid mostly sleep together."

Gabriella had improved a little by the time they got back to the small apartment Adam had rented. Tom considered the extra money he was given with an unexpected solemnity.

"It's all I have," explained Adam.

"It's plenty."

"Where are you from, Tom?"

"Houston."

"Are you going back there?"

"Someplace else I reckon." Tom offered his hand and they shook on it. "The last shuttle goes at the end of the week."

"We'll hang around here for a bit I think. She wouldn't survive the trip home."

"Or the stay," Tom concluded and let himself out.

Adam went into the kitchen and prepared the picnic hamper. He dressed Gabriella before she woke and fitted some cheap sim-shades over her eyes. He put the other pair on, carried Gabriella into the recreation room and laid her on the white, cushioned flooring. The simulation was called Wildwood and was all he could afford.

When Gabriella woke, she sat up unsteadily and looked around. Dappled sunlight came through the leaves of a majestic, old, oak tree. It danced across her face as the branches rustled in the slight breeze. A bee droned past and she reached for it weakly.

"*A la casa*?" she asked.

"Yes, home." Adam came across the clearing and sat beside her. "Gabriella, it's me: Adam … Do you remember me?"

She stared blankly at him for a moment, "*Cabrones!*" she said and then continued looking around the wood.

He forced himself to look at her face. An old, badly stitched scar stretched from her right temple to the opening of her mouth and another ran over the bridge of her nose. The skin was almost translucent: a map of despair clinging to the bones out of habit.

"You were right … It *was* a piecrust promise. But I didn't break it."

"*Cabrones,*" she repeated without feeling.

"I am." He held her hand and despite himself, felt sickened by the bones sliding under the loose skin, by the smell of her. "If love is guilt then I have always loved you, Gabriella."

She smiled, as though he were something of only limited

interest. He couldn't think of anything else to say. After all that lost time … twenty years of sleepwalking through his life, taking any drug he could, lying out in the scrub most nights, just staring at the moon and wondering; there was no way of converting all that into something worth saying, something that could take it all back, free her and absolve him. So he adjusted the remote. The sound of children's laughter came from just beyond the trees. Gabriella turned towards the voices.

"Look," Adam said. "It's the children."

She made a noise and tried to rise.

"No, stay there. I'll call them. Jane! Michael! Come over here!"

They came from behind a tree as if pushed onto a stage. The girl looked to be around five, the boy seven. He swung a stick and his younger sister carried a jam jar full of assorted insects. She held it up as they approached.

"Look what I caught for you, Mummy."

Adam touched the remote again and they went to their mother. The sun burned through the swaying branches. A wood pigeon cooed nearby. Gabriella sat on the blanket with her children and took food from the hamper. She didn't seem to notice that the dried fruit and meat she gave them kept falling through their hands. After some time, Adam took out a bottle and a metal spoon. He poured a viscous red liquid onto the spoon and put it to Gabriella's lips.

"Come along; a spoonful of sugar makes the medicine go down."

Gabriella swallowed it without comment. Adam's hands shook as he poured a spoonful for himself. He felt drowsy very quickly and put his arm around Gabriella's thin waist. She flinched a little and then rested her head upon his shoulder.

"You are slow," Gabriella whispered sleepily.

"I am," Adam replied.

They lay back on the sun-splashed blanket and closed their eyes. The children stood up and stared at the couple, shuffling their feet as they waited for further instructions.

★ ★ ★

… Moises sat up and wiped the tears from his eyes. *Gabriella! Was he seeing her future? Mama selva, what was this magic?*

He was incredibly thirsty and with his mind still struggling over what he had read, he scrabbled around in his rucksack. He found half a bottle of water and as he drained it, his ears picked up a tiny creak from outside. Moises turned in his chair and remained very still, eyes focussed on the indistinct shape of the front door. It had sounded like the wooden steps to his house, bending under a carefully placed foot. He waited. The silence stretched and then as he released a breath it came again! Moises shot out of his chair and ran to the door. When he pulled it open, Walter was halfway up the steps in a crouched position. He looked up, startled, and began to bluster, "Oh, Moises, I thought I heard a call from your house. Thought you might be ill … You said you were ill earlier …"

Moises closed the door behind him.

"I did not hear anything. I am well," he said.

The old man rubbed his ears. "My hearing plays tricks at my age I think."

Moises raised his fist and stepped forward as if about to strike the old man.

"No tricks, why are you here?"

Walter raised his arms to defend his head. "I wondered, I mean the butterfly, do you have it?"

"*Mana intindinichu?*" Moises asked in Quechua. "Señor Dollie? You have contacted him tonight haven't you?"

Walter's eyes widened. A great excitement shone in them. "I knew it! You have the butterfly-"

"Why did you tell him?"

"Señor Dollie said I would be famous."

Moises sighed. "Why does everybody want to be famous these days?" He asked the question quietly, rhetorically.

Walter grinned. "Everybody wants to be famous."

"Go away," said Moises. "If I hear you near my door before he arrives, I will kill you."

Walter backed away into the darkness and his grin was the last thing to disappear. Moises went back inside and bolted the door, rested his head against it for a moment. There was nowhere to run to now. This night would be his last, and it would be endless. He sat and looked down the microscope again …

# SOMEBODIES

Propped against the empty kitchen cupboards, the 40-inch television glowed with sharp, saturated images, its fat-gummed screen jumping to a shapeless dance track. Ascención rested her cereal bowl on the pile of lifestyle magazines that seemed to be the only things holding the TV in place and poured some milk. She took the bowl and sat opposite the two suited gentlemen who were waiting patiently.

"It's the children I worry about mostly. What would be for the best?" she asked loudly, cramming a large spoonful of Pop Tart cereal into her mouth. The music seemed to increase in volume and urgency to compete with her, and she gave the television a disparaging look.

The tall, young man across the table glanced at his older partner and smiled. "That is entirely up to you, Mrs–"

"What?"

"I said that it–"

"Whoar wud ou eccomend?" She shouted through a mouthful of cereal, a little of which landed on the table in front of her. She flicked it away casually.

The man glanced at the TV and smiled an even sunnier smile. "Could we just ..." His hand turned a make-believe dial. "Just a little."

"Sure." Ascención snapped up a remote and pressed it.

"Thanks. That is a nice TV by the way. What I was saying was that, well, the English have a phrase for this, *sin dolor no hay ganancia*, do you understand?"

"Yes, of course." Ascención dropped her spoon in the bowl and sighed. No pain no gain. That was easy for them to say in their shiny suits. What pain had they suffered? She leaned over to peer into the living room. The children were hooked up to their Playplaces, grunting and spitting in frustration. She lowered her voice. "It's a big decision to make on a Saturday morning." She laughed a little. "Haven't woken up yet."

The older man moved a pile of food-encrusted plates aside and slid some brochures across the table. "It is a big decision Ascención, and you only get one shot at it. That's why it's very important you get it right." He put a hand on his colleague's shoulder and his smile increased in wattage. "Young Luis here is correct. The harder it is for your family to endure, the better the results; that is the bottom line. In my opinion, from five years' experience in the business, if you're going to do it, do it properly – no half measures." He leaned back in his chair and waited as Ascención flicked through the brochures. The pictures were glossy and vivid, the testimonials predictably gushing.

"We realise at the high end it appears very expensive, but–"

"It's not about the money; I've been saving for a couple of years now ... I just want it to be long lasting."

The man looked around the kitchen, at the door-less food cupboards and the rashes of damp where the emulsion had bubbled from the walls. "Of course."

Ascención lit up a bacon-flavoured cigar and her visitors pretended not to notice her shaking hand.

"The people from Longlegends™ guaranteed two years newsworthy but you only guarantee six months, and they're cheaper," she said.

The salesmen smiled at each other. The older man spoke again. "It's impossible for them to guarantee two years and in our opinion–"

"Longlegends™ are the biggest in the industry so they must be doing something right." Ascención was pleased at how business-like she sounded now. She had learned quickly that these people were essentially all the same. Their sales talk was full of traps and she was proud of how she had danced around their words that week, trying to find the best deal for her family. Within a few minutes, they usually realised she was no *cojuda* and stopped patronising her.

"Their prices are low because they are a bigger company, but you lose the personal touches because of that, señora. You take a chance with them. Sometimes their work is good, sometimes it's poor. They have been known to carry out the order at the wrong address."

"Yes, I heard about that."

The man shrugged. "Ascención, you are just a number to them, believe me. To us, you are a family of individuals and will be treated with the care and attention you deserve. If you decide to go with ForeverinLights™, we will spend a lot of time getting to know you; that's how we get spectacular results. Your history, your situation and your personalities will enrich the story and give it longevity."

That's what had been worrying Ascención. Was her family interesting enough? Was their story outstanding, their loss so heart-breaking it would stand out from all the others? Ascención took one last tug on her cigar and dropped it into her cereal bowl. "Longevity is the key here," she muttered, as if to herself, "and documentaries, candle-lit vigils."

"It's all here in this brochure, Ascención. This is a growing industry… although it can only grow so far, for obvious reasons. More than ever, the story has to be believable and compelling, otherwise it's not newsworthy. That's where we excel. The more you pay of course, the more you get."

"It's not about the money."

"Of course it isn't. It's about what's best for your family."

The men from ForeverinLights™ let themselves out.

"*A su madre!* I've scrimped and scraped for five years; of course it's about the fucking money," Ascención muttered when she heard the door shut. A cockroach scuttled out from underneath the fridge. She eyed it for a second, threw her cereal bowl and scored a direct hit, cutting the insect in half. The front of the insect righted itself and limped on through the shards of glass and milk. Ascención went over, hunkered down and watched until it gave up the fight for life.

She went back to the table and spent another fifty minutes poring over the shiny brochures. After much consideration, she chose ForeverinLights™ and the Gold B option. As expected, the Platinum range was well out of their financial reach. Looking through the brochure, it was obvious why it was so expensive. There was a more elaborate backstory in the Platinum range, greater attention to detail and even more avenues explored to achieve long-lasting publicity. When Ascención read through the details, her heart yearned for it, but along with the extras, there was the expectation of more sacrifices from the family involved. Some of that she could barely read, let alone consider doing. Take Platinum A for example, the most expensive on the list; it took a whole year to complete!

No, all in all, Gold B was probably the best option for them. They would be part of a serial, which should help. And cameras could be fitted in the house for the duration, which would shave a bit off the cost. She couldn't quite bring herself to opt for Gold A; not right to expect her children to suffer through weeks of it, she supposed.

At just before midday, Ascención put the brochure in the sink and it burst briefly into an intense ball of white flame. She glanced at the clock; it was exactly one hour after she had opened it as they said it would be. They covered their tracks these people. It reassured her to know that.

Her husband, Sergio, was as unsure and half-hearted as he generally was. She approached him with the laptop after he had taken his MAYK-M that afternoon.

"About the kids? Are you sure it is best for them, too?" His red eyes quivered like jellyfish abandoned by a receding tide.

Ascención gave Esteban and Claudia a look; they were both online, eating their lunch with the screens down over their eyes. She had shaved a few extra slivers of MAYK-M topping onto their pizzas and they were buzzing as loudly as the old fridge she couldn't wait to leave behind.

"Do you know how many people have been born on this planet?"

Sergio shrugged. "When?"

"Ever?"

He shrugged again.

"One hundred and six point five billion, and less than one percent of those have been famous for anything."

"*A su*, when you put it like that, but …"

"What?"

"Well, maybe the kids will be famous for doing something when they grow up?"

"There's more chance of us finding the next black butterfly on the indoor garden. Do you want them to be one of the billions forgotten?"

He put down his pizza and picked up the laptop. "Where do I sign?"

They had a month now to make sure everything was right.

The day before the men from ForeverinLights™ were due to come was a short one. Ascención kept looking at the clock as it zipped around. She wanted to physically grab the second hand and hold it still, to have a few moments outside of time where she could not feel the clock relentlessly nudging her into the future.

Everybody has nerves, she reasoned.

Ascención had done all she could to ensure the success of their story; they all had something to lose now. And somehow, even though these things were possibilities created by her own planning, they made it harder for her to let go.

Having successfully begun weaning himself off MAYK-M during the past month, Sergio had got an interview with the newly formed company Hero™, who produced the substitute he was using. Hero™ were making a new, long-running advertisement string, which would follow six users from Cuzco: three who used their product, EEZ-ME, and three who used a rival but unnamed substitute. The company were hoping that the three users of the rival product would fail by going back on MAYK-M. This meant, of course, that the three who were chosen to use their own product, had to succeed. Sergio was subjected to psychological and physical tests to ascertain his suitability. The job came with a new car and rent-free accommodation in the suburbs for the duration of the campaign run, which might be up to six months.

Despite pestering the company at Ascención's urging, Sergio hadn't heard if he had got the position as yet. If it came out afterwards that he had, she knew that could only help.

The children were put through an elaborate array of tests and the possibility of Esteban being a mathematical genius was forecast, while Claudia had a great ear for music. Ascención had paid a violin teacher to assert that Claudia could almost certainly develop into a master violinist. She had a lesson every day for three weeks, despite the fact that she hated it.

Ascención herself was everything she needed to be in that month leading up to the big day. She had timed her pregnancy to perfection and would be eight months when the time came.

It was a little boy and in quiet moments, she would pat her belly and whisper, "You're going to be famous baby," and she would cry a little.

Every weekday afternoon, she did voluntary work with under-privileged children. She found them weak and cloying, but stuck to the task admirably, becoming quite well-liked in a community she had previously tried to escape from.

When she put her own children to bed that night she gave them a cuddle – a rare gift, and they sensed something was different.

"Is tomorrow the special day?" Esteban asked.

"Yes, baby."

"Are we going somewhere?"

"Yes, we are, if you behave that is."

Claudia sat up. "Where to?"

"To a place that will make us famous."

Claudia laughed.

"You want to be somebody, don't you?"

"Yes, Mummy."

"Good, then settle down and get to sleep."

Ascención went to bed alone. She had allowed Sergio some MAYK-M because he couldn't sleep and he had then insisted on spending the night in the children's room.

At around midnight, she had a wild urge to grab the kids and run. She sat up in bed and breathed deeply in the darkness, whispering the reasons for their decision. She was under no illusions. These occurrences were becoming more common, but still … even if it was only for a couple of weeks, or less; they would still rise up through the dismal sea of the nameless, the faceless, and her family would shine in high definition for the briefest of moments. She laid her head back down and watched the brittle glow of the digital alarm clock as it winked through the minutes. She smiled through chattering teeth as she imagined her own face on the big TV in the kitchen, people discussing her story, bringing flowers to her house …

A blinding light and a shriek of terror woke her. The scream was hers: a pre-emptive strike against what she knew was coming.

Two men in grey clothing were in her bedroom. Their faces had been wiped. Sergio was crawling in front of them. One of the men swung a boot up into his stomach and he rolled over, mewling like a sick cat. His hands clawed at the trousers of the man who had kicked him and red spittle bubbled from his mouth. There was a crunch as the boot met his face again and a bright loop of blood swung across the duvet near Ascención's feet.

The men chuckled, but their featureless faces hardly moved.

Sergio got to his knees and waved his hands around blindly, trying to find his assailant. Ascención could see why; the men had the children, one each under the left arm while the right ran a chromium blade back and forth through the gauzy air. The man who held Claudia addressed Ascención; his voice came hot and muffled from the small mouth and the children were sobbing so it took a couple of seconds for her brain to decipher his words.

"We were told to offer you Option A at a slightly reduced rate," he said breathlessly, "better chance of longevity for the story."

Ascención opened her mouth but nothing happened.

"Come on: A or B?"

"B," she whispered.

"Okay, thanks for choosing Foreverinlights™." He put Claudia down, pulled her head back and placed the knife blade against the galloping pulse in her throat. Ascención lurched out of bed screaming. For the first time in as long as she could remember, she didn't want to be famous.

★ ★ ★

… Moises jerked his head up, dragged back to the reality of the hut by the sound of the door breaking open behind him. He rubbed his eyes and turned to see three silhouettes melt into the darkness as the door shut behind them.

"Señor Dollie?" Moises whispered.

"It is, and these here fellas are Garcia and Isaacs. You're fixing to damage your eyes reading under such an inadequate light."

Moises could just make out the big man's lips moving in the gloom.

"That is a magnificent creature. Why didn't you bring it straight to me and collect your reward? You deserve every Sol."

The other two men had flanked Moises casually. His stomach tightened. "I was tired."

Dolly stood over the table and whistled in admiration. "I wondered if we'd ever get it, I got to admit. What a sight." He leaned closer to the butterfly, his lips moving silently as he studied it. He fingered the pins holding the wings in place and turned his head to take in the microscope and the books. His voice hardened. "What have you been doing?"

Moises said nothing.

"Well, I reckon to have around twelve thousand butterflies in my collection. I know a lepidopterist when I see one and you ain't it. That shit-heel Hawthorne filled your head with nonsense, didn't he? Got you thinking ideas above your station."

"*Mama selva, dame fuerza!*"

"Still calling for Pachamama's help? You gotta help yourself in this world, boy. Get up and stretch your legs a piece."

Moises got up and one of the men ushered him away from the table. The other sat down and put his eyes to the microscope. He moved the head around and adjusted the zoom a few times.

"Nothing," he said without bringing his head up, "nothing at all."

"Go get some decent light will you, Isaacs?"

The man at the microscope got up and left the hut. Before the door swung shut, Moises caught a glimpse of a group of soldiers, guns slung across their chests, waiting in the street. Walter was standing with them. Dollie seated himself at the table and looked down the microscope, tutting and sighing as he adjusted the zoom. Eventually, he sat up and clasped his hands, his eyes roving over the giant insect like centipedes searching for hidden worms.

They waited.

Mosquitos spun in the tiny halo of light. There was just Dollie's slow, heavy breathing, the faint purr of the cicada in the forest outside and Moises's heart thumping dark panic through his chest.

Isaacs returned with two battery-powered lanterns. He placed one on the table and hung the other from the roof strut above the door. Dollie turned to Moises, his face thrown into a chiaroscuro by the lantern beside him. He smiled. "Walter says you been in here for upwards of three hours, making less noise than a church mouse pissing into a ball of cotton wool."

"I was looking at the butterfly. She is beautiful."

Dollie gave it a glance as if to check. "How many stories are on there?"

"Stories?"

"You look plum wore out; you must've read a few?"

Moises wiped his mouth with the back of his hand. Dollie took another look through the microscope and sighed. "Why you? What's so special about Moises that only he can read the black butterfly? Remind me; where you from? Lima? Cuzco?"

"*Bagua. La masacre.*"

"That was no massacre," Dollie muttered, still studying the

butterfly. "Besides, Emerald Earth was there for you in your darkest hour, gave you a paying job. You never thought to remember that?"

"Where is Hawthorne?"

"I wouldn't fret about him." Dollie stood up and gestured to the chair he had vacated. "Sit down here, Moises. Tell me about your day … everything mind."

Moises spent the next twenty minutes doing just that. Dollie's questions became sharper and less methodical as the minutes ticked by.

"It can't be a coincidence, can it? This reserve covers close on two hundred and fifty thousand acres and the butterfly happens to drop down right in front of your sorry ass." He ran a hand through his short, salt and pepper hair, and ordered Garcia to get them all a drink. "But you are a peculiar animal," he said as he watched Moises drain a bottle of water and sat down beside him. The look on his face was quite genial now and he spoke as if he were conducting an informal interview. "I know all about you, Moises. You read books, you paint and you are always at that crummy cinema in Iquitos when allowed to: you and that pederast Hawthorne cosying up under the silver screen, eh?" Dollie tapped his fingers on the wooden table top. "You ain't no average Indian, I'll give you that. You're like a fucking sponge."

Moises shrugged.

"Read me a story, Quispé."

"I–"

"Don't tell me you can't see them, cuz I know you can. I just don't know why or how. Quispé means glass in Quechua don't it? Well, I can see right through you, so fess up."

Moises shook his head. His right hand went to the pocket in his shorts and felt the hard lump of the matchbox there; he wanted his gum. His legs began to shake.

The big Texan gave an almost imperceptible nod and Garcia

grabbed Moises's arms from behind. Dollie took the boy's left hand and smashed it down on the table top repeatedly until Moises opened his fist. Then, putting his weight on Moises's wrist with his left arm, Dollie brought out a short, deep-bladed knife and forced it into the gap between the boy's third and last finger.

Moises waited for the question to come again but instead, Dollie rolled the knife with a grunt of effort and swept the finger off the table. A pitiful howl filled the little hut and for a second, Moises wondered who had made it. Shock rolled through his body and his vision faded. An enormous white pain erupted in his hand. It soared through his senses and he realised with terror that it wasn't going to stop growing. And then it was past what he could bear and he no longer had control of his body. He jumped around on the chair, sucking in air, waving his arm about and whipping blood across the floor.

Without a word, Dollie grabbed the arm again and steadied it as Moises screamed. Isaacs dressed the stump of the little finger tightly. The bandages bloomed red immediately and began to drip steadily onto the table. Then Garcia stuck a needle through Moises's thin shirt and into his upper arm.

"Aside your thumb, that's the most important finger on your hand." Dollie was shaking as he pointed at the hut floor. "Most your hand's strength is in that little finger. Hold it up, boy. Hold it up or you'll lose too much." His teeth shone as he moved through the lantern light. "Feels like you've got it stuck in a mound of fire ants don't it? The morphine will take the edge off pretty soon."

Moises rocked back and forth, unable to fix a coherent thought. He was making little mewling noises, which came despite his attempts to stop them. Dollie left the hut for twenty minutes, but it felt like hours to Moises. While he was gone, Garcia mopped up the blood from the table and wrapped even more bandage around Moises's hand. It was a bloody stump now.

When Dollie returned, he drew a chair up in front of Moises and lifted the boy's chin. "I hate all this violence, to be straight. But I'll take everything from you if I have to. You know that, don't you? Your eyes and tongue go last, cuz I need them. Read me a story Quispé … I been waiting a long time."

Moises wiped his nose with his good hand and went back to the eyepieces. A pulse of dull pain was spreading up his arm and his hand felt like it was moving to the beat. Beneath the throb, spiky streaks of a bigger pain moved, occasionally piercing through the morphine's defences.

"You are not a god," Moises said as he refocused the microscope. "You are tiny, this world is tiny …" His face contorted with frustration. He couldn't find the words.

Dollie smiled good-naturedly. "You're a real treat, you know that? How many stories can you see?"

"Hundreds."

Dollie blew a whistle of excitement. "So first of all, read me the ones you read before I arrived."

"I cannot; they are gone after I read them."

"Really?" He eyed the boy carefully. "I believe you, but I don't like it much." He took out a Dictaphone and clicked it on. "Read."

Moises Quispé began to speak …

# SEA CELL

It is said that the brain looks for patterns in what it sees, in an effort to make sense of the insensible. Occasionally, I entertain the comforting notion that I was supposed to go down to the beach that day, that it was a lesson, or a message of some sort. But that is a sentiment left over from before, like a singed photograph found in a burnt-out church.

I don't believe in God anymore; at least not the one I believed in back then. If there is a God then he is as blind to our concerns as we are to the bacteria that swarm over and through our bodies.

The warnings were daubed across the clinic doors again that Tuesday afternoon in red paint that had run like horror film blood:

*LAZARRO GO HOME*

I had been out for an hour and a half, picking up some milk and vegetables donated by the Catholic Church up on the hill at Santa Marcha. I put my finger to the letters. The paint was soft, skinned over by the strong wind coming off the Pacific Ocean. Beneath it, up against the doors, two tousle-haired boys sat wrapped in a coarse brown blanket. There were spots of red paint drying on it. These people did this while the two boys, abandoned, homeless, were sitting beneath them. I told myself that they didn't know any better, that Lima was full of children like this; they were as common and as unnoticed as stray dogs.

I took the two boys in and gave them some oatmeal. "Didn't

you notice these two, or the people who painted the doors again?" I asked Sara, the head nurse.

She looked up from the stove where she was shuffling steaming saucepans, at the early stages of preparing food for fifty-two children.

"I did not know the little ones were out there. I heard the others, yes; how could I not? Shouting their obscenities... *hijoputas!*" She spat the insult. "But Elenor had gone home ..." She moved a pan and turned, pushed her hands down her apron and raised her chin. "What was I to do, Señor Lazarro?"

"Nothing I guess, Sara."

Her eyes were blazing now. "Nothing? Are you sure? Maybe I should attack them with this hot water" – she gestured at the stove – "leave the children and start a war on the street, huh?"

"No," I said. "I am sorry I was not here."

Sara nodded. "I am sorry, too."

I put the food and milk away and took the children into the ground-floor examination room. She was a proud woman and she didn't need to say sorry. We were all sorry here, for one reason or another. More often than not, lately, I was sorry for starting this, bringing my wife, Maria, here, having a child here. Nina was a year old. Should she be brought up in this place? Why not? Was she more important than the children I found on the doorstep? Of course she was. That was the problem; I had started to think differently about it all.

Both the boys were malnourished. One of them, Victor, was blind in one eye because of a tumour. After some probing, I found out they were brothers, five and four years old. I made some notes and took them upstairs. The building was filled with the sounds of running feet, crying, shouting and the occasional burst of laughter: children bouncing around like microbes reacting to tiny stimuli. I heard the phone chirping downstairs and waited for my name to be called.

"Señor Lazarro?"

"I'll take it up here, Sara." I squatted next to the boys. "Go downstairs and play with the other boys and girls. I will be down soon."

Big, dark eyes looked back at me, unsure of my sincerity.

"Go on, you will be fine."

Victor put his arm around his brother and they turned away and moved slowly toward the stairs.

I took the call in my study on the first floor.

"*Hola!* Miguel Lazarro. How can I help?"

"*Buenos dias*, Señor Lazarro. It is Anthony Hawthorne of Emerald Earth. I have been instructed to contact all of the orphanages we have previously done business with, regarding adding new faces to our programme."

"Oh, haven't you enough already?"

The Englishman laughed, as if embarrassed. "Well, our project continues to grow, and it's a big jungle Señor Lazarro, we do misplace a few of our employees from time to time."

"How do you mean, 'misplace'?"

"They leave without telling us, have accidents sometimes; it's hard to keep track of everyone." He laughed again.

I wanted to reach down the phone line and squeeze his neck with all my strength. I had met Hawthorne once before, just after Emerald Earth had first contacted us. I didn't like the way he looked at the children, at the boys to be exact.

"These are children you are talking about."

"I know. It's sad–"

"They are in your custody; you should be taking more care of them."

"We do, we do! They are paid well, educated, fed; unfortunately the world is not perfect, señor."

I didn't reply. I willed myself to put the phone down before he came to the offer, but, shamefully, I did not.

"We need at least another hundred: ten from you would be great. Two eyes, no deformities that would hinder them physically or mentally really. We are offering four hundred Nuevo Sol per boy. That's twice what we paid you–"

"I know, I know." The calculation flashed through my mind before I could stop it. Four thousand Nuevo Sol, give or take: enough to pay the rent on this big, old house for the next six months. I listened to my wheedling voice as it made its pitiful demands, merely a sop to my conscience, which huddled in the darkness.

"If I agree, I need assurances that these children are okay, to get word from them from time to time; otherwise, it's no deal."

"Of course. We always encourage them to do that, Señor Lazarro. You have my word on that. Don't you receive letters at the moment?"

"Sometimes."

"Good, we will be in the area in two weeks from today. I will ring you nearer the time. Have we a deal?"

"Maybe. I will see if I have any suitable."

I placed the phone on the cradle and put my head in my hands. My fingers gripped my cheeks, pressing into the flesh. I felt the nails threatening to break the skin and made an agonised sound, low and mournful. Fifty children I had given over to Emerald Earth in the past two years, two hundred Nuevo Sol a piece, and I had no real idea of their situation now. It was true that I did receive letters occasionally, but they looked to be run from the same template, something that had always bothered me. Perhaps the children were helped with the writing of the letters; that would be natural, wouldn't it? I wasn't doing anything wrong here, only my best to run this place, to look after and nourish those in my care, to keep it all running on an inadequate budget. I couldn't be responsible for the children after they left me, could I?

I stood up, feeling claustrophobic all of a sudden. I thought about going upstairs to see Maria and Nina, but I just couldn't face it for some reason. Then, quite suddenly, I didn't want to be there anymore. I hurried downstairs and out through the paint-splashed doors before anyone could stop me. Soon, I was on the Pan Pacific Highway in my little Toyota minivan heading south, without a clear thought in my head.

It was around four thirty when I set off, and the sun was slipping down the western sky, eager to be doused by the ocean. There was no sign of the usual mist, hadn't been for a few days. November was dying and summer was close. I lowered the window and smelt the ocean. I had no idea where I was going, but I was driving too fast. The cars droning past going the opposite way seemed to soothe me strangely, like a lullaby played through combustion. I focussed only on what was ahead through the rectangle of angled glass. The road flashing under me, my right hand at twelve o'clock, knuckles like a range of tiny hills above it, capped in white as too much pressure was applied to the steering wheel.

After a few minutes, I saw the big blue sign for Miraflores and jerked the wheel to the left, cutting someone off. The wail of protesting horns sailed away on the highway above as I pulled off and coasted to a stop by a set of tennis courts. A middle-aged couple in pastel colours were running back and forth along the baselines, trading shots. I wound the window up, lay my head back and sighed. The tick of the cooling engine soothed me now, tapping gently in the relative silence.

In this silence away from the house, I had a new perspective on things. It had been a long day after all and they were always long days: up before five to check on the children, get the windows open and turn on the water pump; the house cleaned early, so by seven everyone is eating breakfast; then my rounds of the city hospitals. These trips were always mentally wearing;

that morning I had visited a girl who had knocked on my door last week, wheezing and grey at six years old. Tuberculosis, untreated for years, had eaten most of her right lung away. Situations like this were fairly common, unremarkable even. And yet I still asked myself how it could be. I couldn't disassociate myself from these kids.

I just needed a break. When did I last have a break? It was a ridiculous question. There was no such thing as a break, only in the magazines I sometimes read in the hospital waiting rooms.

This *was* the break I thought. Meagre though it was, an hour or two would surely help. I would get some fresh air, go for a walk on the beach and then head back, hopefully with my mind a little clearer. As if in response to these thoughts, my cell phone began to vibrate in my pocket. It was Maria. I sent her a text, reassuring her of my safety and put it back in my pocket, ignoring the ping of her reply.

I walked through an industrial unit and found myself on a quiet access road that curled down the hill above the sandstone cliffs. Before long, there was a fork in the headland and the Pacific opened out before me. The sun was almost touching it now: a white disc bleeding hazy yellows into the distant water. Above me, the broken cloud had darkened, shot through with silver and deep violet, dirty greys. The wind was cool and absentminded, unable to remember which way it wanted to blow. There had been a big storm the day before and the memory of its violence still tainted the air. I stood, hands in pockets for a few moments, my hair swirling around my face, watching tiny whitecaps break far out on the friendless ocean. I felt better already.

I chose to go right and the cliff fell away quickly. There was a rough stairway, which zig-zagged down it, sometimes in the teeth of the wind, where I found myself shrinking into the uneven cliff wall behind me, the sandstone crumbling beneath my feet. Then the steps would turn behind shivering trees and I would stop for a few moments in the relative silence and catch my breath. It felt peculiar, as if I were lost and the rest of the world had planned it that way. But I didn't mind. I wanted to be lost for a while.

By the time I reached the base of the cliff, I was wondering if I should have taken the other track. This one seemed unused; I had seen nobody since I left the road. I came out from behind a soft, broken boulder that had, sometime previously, fallen from the cliff face. It was a small, enclosed beach of large, uneven pebbles. Across the bay, strings of yellow lights hung across the tourist area of the Miraflores district.

The beach was around 40 yards across and signs of the previous day's storm were very apparent. Pieces of flotsam were strewn about it, heaps of glossy seaweed, trembling jellyfish, wind-rippled and effortlessly alien. The sea was still throwing itself at the shore with some force, like an enormous creature trying to drag itself up onto the land. I listened to the fizz of the surf and the deep rumble as thousands of pebbles were drawn back under its weight.

My eyes were drawn to her.

She was just above the surf-line and for a moment I thought that what I was looking at was a dead seal or a stranded porpoise. Instinctively, I looked back the way I had come, then upwards, shielding my eyes as I searched the sheer face of the cliff above me. There was nobody else around.

Out of the corner of my eye, I glimpsed movement and turned too quickly. The slick pebbles shifted under me with a grinding noise and I stumbled, just managing to stay on my feet. A gull, blown over my head by a gust of wind, mocked me again and again.

I walked over to the naked body. *It had rolled over hadn't it?*

She was lying on her back now. I stood behind her, looking

85

down on her bald head. Her arms lay by her side neatly, palms up. The tide was going out. It rattled the pebbles just beyond her swollen feet and drained away with a hiss.

I took a wide walk around her so I could view her face the right way up. My heart dropped into my stomach. *My God! How long had she been in the ocean?* Her stomach was distended, filled with water I guessed. Her legs and arms were thin and sunken, the bones gleaming through the translucent skin like flickering light bulbs in the failing light.

I took out my phone and looked at it for a moment. What was I waiting for? It was five thirty; night would fall within the hour. I put the phone back in my pocket and knelt down beside her. Was it a she after all? I looked back at her crotch in embarrassment. There was nothing down there, not even hair – no hair on her body at all in fact. Did hair fall out in sea water?

I felt a heavy sadness overtake me and realised that I didn't want to share this feeling with anyone else, not yet anyway. She was so alone. I wondered about her history: where she was from and what she did for a living; all the minutiae of her life leading up to this moment that must have seemed so important while it was happening, but meant absolutely nothing now. Her face, upon closer inspection, appeared ageless; maybe the salt water had worn away any wrinkles. Her eyes had rolled back. They were tinged with green like over-boiled eggs. There was no jewellery on her, no tattoos on her skin, no scars, not a hint at her personality or identity. She lay before me, grey on grey, an unfinished sculpture by an artist who may have fled before my arrival, unnerved by what he might create if he continued.

As my eyes struggled in the dismal light, the body seemed to lose all of its humanity. Now it was just a bloated shape, something utterly abstract. I stood up, shocked at how my mind was re-evaluating what I was seeing. I felt disgusted at myself; surely she had just been in the water too long.

It was time to ring *la policia*, but before I did, I knelt down again and laid my hand on her shoulder. I had a romantic idea that it would be a chivalrous thing to do, a caring thing, that I was being sensitive and thoughtful. It was just a tiny movement, a moment among millions I have experienced, and I would give anything to take it back.

It convulsed at my touch.

I jumped back and rolled away from the thing as water pulsed from what I had thought was the mouth. The sound of the wind turned my scream into something small and pitiful, shook it and tossed it away. The cold ocean hit my hands and knees and stunned me. I stood up, unable to pull my eyes away from that grey shape wheezing in the thickening darkness. I ran my tongue over my lips, comforted by the salt thrown up in a fine mist by the breaking waves. I could not move.

Time passed. I expected the creature to crawl over to me and drag me back with it to the bottom of the ocean. But the minutes continued to tick by without any further movement from the thing, and my mind drifted with the tide. When I was washed back up into clear thought, I was in total darkness. There was just the shout and the whisper of the sea, alternating its mood by the moment: relentless, immutable. And the pebbles answering ... clack ... clack ... clack.

My paralysis broke suddenly. I ran from the beach, fell down a dozen times and nearly slipped from the cliff a dozen more. I didn't register the pain or the fear of my flight from the beach until afterwards; didn't feel safe until I got to my Toyota and pulled away with a screech of tyres.

I didn't ring the police or tell Maria or anyone else about what I had discovered. I knew that once I started telling the tale, I would be unable to stop myself from sharing the most important part of it and nobody was going to accept that. Because it wasn't a body I found down on that beach that night, of a woman or a man or anything else. It's difficult to know how to put it into words. When I placed my hand on that thing's flesh, I didn't see, I just understood, and it happened in a microsecond. Something passed from it to me: knowledge so enormous that I often wonder if it came at all.

I sensed that it was a cell. An image reared in my mind for a fraction of a second: the ocean like a giant parasite, clinging to another organism, the earth perhaps, and that spinning through the internals of a yet much vaster organism ... a God? I felt there was much more but my hand came away instinctively and my mind retreated with it. I don't think it meant to communicate. I'm not even sure it was aware of me in any sense we would understand. The insight just came to me naturally, like picking up a germ or something. There was no sense of wonder. It was cold and thoughtless.

There are nearly nine million people in Lima, all scurrying around, battering their heads together. There are thousands of homeless children, even more confused than the adults: cold and lost and unloved. I still try to help some of them as best I can. But I have lost some compassion, and it was destroyed by, of all things, empathy.

I rang Emerald Earth the next day, told them they could have the children, and that I would continue to supply them in the future. It doesn't seem so important anymore, any of it.

Sometimes I sit downstairs in the communal living room with the children running around me and I think about that thing on the beach, on how it got dragged up from somewhere it should never have left. I wonder if it went back or like a glob of snot from somebody's nose, it just dried up and died. And watching my daughter, Nina, crawling around the room on all fours, making her funny little noises, I think about those microscope slides they show on science programmes sometimes and it makes me feel different about her, different about my wife and also about myself.

And I want to be sick.

# EMPTY HEAVEN

The room commenced its awakening programme: raising the temperature by 1.8 degrees and filtering soft, vitamin-enriched light through the organic walls. The cool smell of dew-laden meadow grass filled the air and somewhere nearby, a dove cooed a gentle wake-up call. The man on the bed remained asleep.

The room instructed the Bio-MEMS implanted in the man's chest to lower the secretion of melatonin and administer adrenaline. It waited a further ninety seconds before emitting an extremely mild infrasonic wave to gently raise the patient's heartbeat and nudge him into consciousness. After three more minutes, it spoke.

"Good morning, it is Mr Schema. Just confirm by opening your eyes upon your new first day."

The man opened his eyes and sat up. He looked around the room for a few moments and his face showed a quick succession of emotions, as if he were unable to find one that correctly matched his feelings.

"What happened?" He swung his legs out of bed and sank his feet into the layer of heated massage air just above the floor. He tried to stand, passed out for a second and came around as he fell back onto the large bed.

"Please stay still for a few moments while your Harmoniser adjusts and dispenses your prescribed medications. How are you feeling now?" the room asked.

"Oh swell, great, good to be alive and all that other horseshit." The man flinched and slowly sat up. "Why the hell am I talking like this?" He tried to project his mirror image and realising his I-Kno was disconnected, picked up an antique mirror from the bedside table and studied his reflection. He turned his cheek this way and that, probing the teeth with his fingers, pulling at his eyelids so that he could see the wet, scarlet sockets beneath. "I feel strange," he murmured. "What happened to me?"

"After breakfast, your doctor will explain—"

"You explain."

"We are unable by law to—"

"Sure, sure! Spare me the whisperprint."

When the room had finished its monologue, he complained again about the way he was talking. "Why is my teller on this crappy factory setting?"

The room apologised on behalf of the hospital and enquired after his chosen vernacular.

"'English Gentleman' of course. It must be on your records. Please do it now; I just said 'swell', for Christ sake."

The room asked the man to lie down and gently put him out. He woke twenty minutes later and sat on the edge of the bed talking to himself. All seemed to be in order: not a 'swell' or a 'horseshit' to be heard.

Breakfast arrived: green algae on toast, mango juice and a sweet, green tea. It was served by a voluptuous nurse who greeted him with a smile that made his stomach quiver. She was a flawless Brasstint.

"Good morning, Amber," he said, reading her name badge.

"Good morning, Mr Daniel Schema. Are you feeling new today?"

"Sex?" he suggested.

Her smile thinned, but only fractionally. "Not in your condition and I don't do physical anyway. I'm not a clone."

"That's tragic."

"I think the word you are looking for is hygienic, Mr Schema."

The nurse laid the tray in front of him and stood quite still for a moment. Her brown eyes flickered a little as the room fed her information on Daniel's condition.

"Uh huh!" She leaned over and pulled open Daniel's shirt to study his chest. Her fingers caressed his skin. "Seems to be fine. You've no pain here have you? We're not detecting any."

"No. Why do I need this?" he asked.

She turned her head, which was very close to him, and he breathed in the sweet scent of her hair.

"It's precautionary. Success depends upon how quickly your body and your mind develop their new relationship. During the first few days, they may struggle to unite, so the Harmoniser acts as a kind of mediator between them, introducing medication when needed, as well as regulating your blood pressure and organ functions. It is just a more sophisticated version of your regular Bio-MEMS. They'll work hand in hand for the time being, but I'm sure you know all this, Mr Schema."

Daniel's smile faded slightly. "What new relationship?"

"Dr Gene-Mart will—"

"I feel high."

"You're not quite yourself at the moment. The infrasonics don't help. Give it a little time."

He sipped at his tea and studied the nurse's face. "Nice Gallo-work, but you're heavier; not sure if I prefer it."

"That's copyright laws; you must leave a significant difference or the real Natalie wouldn't be quite so valuable."

"I'm aware of that. I'm not a fool. How much for your sex-mems?"

"I'll mail you a price list when you're reconnected."

"And clones?"

"I have two, but demand is high at the moment. You may expect a queue."

"How much to jump it?"

"Eat your breakfast, Mr Schema." Amber left him staring at the tray. He picked at the algae in a desultory fashion and spoke to the room. "Well, I don't feel any happier with my condition. Why don't you address my neuroses?"

There was a brief pause.

"We are unable by Life Law at this time to erase or modify any wetware unless specified under the terms of your life insurance agreement."

"Exactly, but I assume from my presence here that you've acted without my permission, which is an infringement of my human rights."

There was another pause.

"It was not an infringement because it was instructed by the terms of your policy."

Daniel picked the mirror back up and angled it around his head. "I want my rights," he said half-heartedly.

"The Life Law states at this time that–"

"You're an idiot!" he said and ate his breakfast.

Dr Gene-Mart came to see him after breakfast. She was young, sixteen at the most, Daniel guessed. She sat opposite him and called up his file.

"Now, Mr Schema, are you aware of your situation?"

"I had an accident of some sort."

The doctor crossed her legs, adjusted her white smock a little and her bronze-tinted skin flashed under the stark lighting as she moved. She peered over her antique, horn-rimmed glasses. They jarred with the otherwise clinical, efficient appearance.

"You committed suicide."

"Attempted."

"Succeeded. We regenerated you under the terms of your life insurance policy."

"But I didn't know–"

"The policy was set up for you by your parents when you were a child. Your memory needs a little more augmentation. You were aware previously and have given your permission for us to update your consciousness file on many occasions."

Daniel picked the mirror up again. He studied his reflection for a moment and then lifted his other hand to check if there was a wrinkle misplaced on his palm.

"My God! I finally found some pluck. How did I do it?"

"I can't divulge that information."

"I can find out when I leave here so why not tell me?"

"It is not within my remit. You may view a recording of the incident once you're outside the hospital, but you cannot re-live it as the memory file no longer exists. This will prevent any unnecessary mental suffering on your part and so enable you to move forward."

"Fuck you!"

"Pardon?"

"You heard me. You can't do this to me. Get an adult in here."

Dr Gene-Mart stood up. "You are under a mental evaluation, sir. I decide when you can leave this building, so I suggest you co-operate."

"Fuck you! You can't keep me here."

"I can and I will, if I think it necessary. Keep the profanities coming, because I'm suing you for every single one. Now there is another matter to go over. Do you know what a memory fold is, Mr Schema?"

"Of course I don't."

"It's not a natural phenomenon. It's caused by a banned drug called Somex. It's a complicated drug; suffice to say that when Somex is taken it covers a real memory with a fake one. We found two memory folds in your previous brain and the authorities are wondering how the folds got there."

"I haven't the slightest idea what you're talking about."

"I know you don't," the doctor sighed.

"So why are you asking me?"

"I'm just following a mandatory procedure set down by the insurance company."

Daniel threw the mirror across the room and it bounced harmlessly off the soft wall. "To hell with them!"

The doctor left the room without another word. Daniel felt the infrasonic wave roll through him and fell back onto the bed.

That evening, Nurse Amber came to see him after dinner. She was wearing a short, diaphanous dress and her body flowed like liquid metal beneath its delicate touch. She sat opposite him and flicked her hair back.

"Good evening, Daniel. I wondered if you might be interested in some extra healthcare?"

"Physical advertising. I've never ... I mean, that is you isn't it?"

"Yes of course."

She came across and stood over him. "I could be no other; your I-Kno isn't fitted yet."

She held her hand in front of his face and he looked up at her. She nodded. Daniel bent forward and kissed her palm. His reflection flashed in the polished skin. She tasted of gingerbread. Keeping her eyes on his bulging groin, she backed away slowly and sat down.

"Now then, proteomic healthcare; we have some exciting new cover."

On the fifth morning, Daniel woke to find a basic Pantone suit hanging from the wall. As he put it on, he became a little apprehensive. His room made some reassurances and he sat down as the Harmoniser reacted to his mood and soothed it.

"When will my I-Kno receiver be fitted?"

"Dr Gene-Mart will supervise fitting herself this morning."

He had experienced dead air only once before. Craving peace, he had disconnected from the Neural Web with an old, steel dinner fork. That agonising memory and the moments following had been saved for him by the hospital, probably to deter him from disconnecting again. He had had only four minutes of remembered disconnection, lying on the floor of his home, still gripping the bloodied fork, waiting for the ambulance his house had called. But beneath the searing pain, he had glimpsed something. Simple thoughts had bloomed in the new, vast silence: clean, precise ideas that settled behind his tear-blurred vision like a flurry of snowflakes. He sensed that they were revelatory, but despite his best efforts, could not recall their content.

Daniel fingered the shunt behind his ear that would take the I-Kno receptor. The hard drive was in there already: a delicate web of gold coils interfacing with his cerebrum, waiting to flicker and sing once he was reconnected. He had thought – hoped – that the profundities might return before that happened. Why hadn't they? For four days now, he had waited for some kind of epiphany, but had felt nothing but the old, dull rage building and then falling - as the Harmoniser reacted - like waves falling on some terribly isolated beach. Something fundamental had changed during regeneration. Despite the silence, despite the emptiness, nothing but anger grew in his mind now.

After fitting and testing his I-Kno, Dr Gene-Mart accompanied him to the exit. Despite throttled bandwidth for the first twelve hours after reconnection, he still felt a truck of data smashing into his senses. His inbox began to fill rapidly with sensitive traffic and he struggled to prioritise responses to the requests/offers/messages as he walked. His mind constructed a holding pattern as flashes of images burned his retina lenses, tastes jumped on his tongue and music echoed down the corridors of his psyche.

He accessed Dr Gene-Mart's 'open' files. She was fourteen years old and already a qualified Nano-Medic and a Memory Augmentation Surgeon. But reading between the data, Daniel could see she came from a flawed gene pool.

*What's it like being yet another Gene-Mart? He thought as they reached the exit.*

*It's perfectly fine, Mr Schema. Some of us do not have the fortune of having gold chip sponsors.*

*How long did it take to get that tint?*

*Five years.*

*Bravo! That's impressive for your age and now you are desperately saving for a silver license.*

*I'm working on it.*

*Good luck! They won't authorise that for another ten years, if ever. It's not just about the credit you know? Silvers are rare for a reason. Most people just don't pass the Genome test.*

Dr Gene-Mart left him at the hospital doors and Daniel reluctantly paged a taxi.

*Taxi for Daniel Schema due to arrive at door* – He leaned back – *twelve of Eternal Hospital at thirteen hundred hours ... It will arrive in two minutes, Mr Schema.*

The doors opened. His cab did not arrive. Daniel mailed a complaint as he pondered what to do. The sensible thing would be to ask for re-entry to the hospital while he waited for another cab. He stood there undecided and some premium ads, alerted to his presence on the street, jostled for his attention.

*Hey, Daniel, ever been to Teotihuacán in 1495 (recreation)*
*during the feast for the Sun God? I know you haven't.*
*Moonlight on the water, all that sex, all that blood and perhaps*
*a chance find while you're there … the Mexican black butterfly*
*(as imagined) … What might you read on her wings?*

*… Revitalise your passion for hate with us, Mr Schema.*
*Celebrities, friends, parents – Allow **us** to allow **you** to kill*
*them (subject to authorisation from individuals concerned) in*
*a dazzling array of methods with our top of the range clones*
*which respond – unlike our competitors' – authentically …*

*… your own real child, guaranteed success with his or her*
*future exactly mapped down to each hour of each day (or*
*introduced spontaneity under your guidance) and with a life*
*expectancy of five years, so you can move on with YOUR life*
*free of stress, but with all the fond memories of love that they*
*gave …*

His tint was beginning to attract a lot of attention. The bandwidth was noisy and chaotic. Spam might have flooded his inbox but his throttled bandwidth spared him. His I-Kno authorised small charitable donations befitting his status and bounced any pleas from individuals. Fifty yards down the road, an old Crawlos ad-mobile harassed a crass Leopardtint, while her children chased the nano-cereals that it spat out into their hands.

Two minutes came and went. Sellers licensed to the area were flooding in now. One was an affiliate of his major life sponsor, Continents Remembered. Daniel was reminded by the virtual of his obligations; he was contractually obliged to take home an African pet. He chose a 4-foot vanilla giraffe. It was a smell he could bear more than most and while he waited for the taxi, the ad told him about his new acquisition.

*... Top of the range, enhanced skills in bestiality ... All regular features included, house trained and able to speak 5,000 words in English and Japanese. Faeces odour to be chosen before delivery ...*

Coconut, he thought.

*Vanilla and coconut are good choices, sir.*

The taxi was six minutes late. There followed a minute of low-level litigation between himself, the hospital (who were nothing but apologetic) and the taxi firm.

As he was getting into the car, the square across the road jumped into light and a 60-foot, platinum-skinned Mahatma Gandhi began to walk as crowds jostled around him.

*Schema International has always been at the forefront of neural development. Now their latest upgrade may allow you to read a person's intentions even when they are censoring or – wait for it! – offline!*

A dark-skinned man brandishing a gun pushed out of the crowd to confront Gandhi, but the yogi already had a pistol pulled from his robes and trained on his would-be assassin. He shot the man and then addressed the body.

*God forgive you, Nathuram Godse.* Gandhi looked up. *If only I had been connected to the Neural Web back in '48, I might have continued my great work* – a large black butterfly alighted on his left shoulder and he smiled at it – *and had a meeting of minds. Upgrade now! It might just save you the cost of regeneration. Praise is to God and Schema International.*

It was the first time Daniel had experienced his father's latest ad on the street. It brought him more unwanted attention. He was inundated with enquiries about the new upgrade as people in the vicinity became aware of his Brandname. He redirected them to the Schema site umbrella, via, of course, his own personal Brandsite and the blog he had updated when his I-Kno had been reconnected that morning.

On a whim, he asked the taxi to drop him on the high street so he could take a short walk to his house. It was a cool afternoon and his suit heated slightly to compensate, turning a particular-branded yellow hue to discourage any offline street thugs: he was too connected to victimise. To his left, the road was clogged with slow-moving traffic. On his right, through the impenetrable line of Ragebush that separated his street from Downtown, he could hear the occasional holler and whoop of some of its citizens as they tried to impress the advertisers. Reluctantly, he contacted his mother.

*Why didn't you come to see me, Mother?*

*I did. I watched you grow for a while; it was quite moving. Your father says he thought I might cry solo at one point ... didn't you, darling? I'm just telling Daniel that you said that I nearly solo cried yesterday evening.*

His dad grunted a thought in the background.

*Yes, Mother, but I meant in person, not online.*

*Why, that's crazy, Daniel. That Gene-Mart girl has kept us up to date.*

*I don't like her; she's a never-be and since when did you speak to anyone below a silver tint?*

*Well, one makes exceptions. She's been very helpful. Anyway, you know it's not safe to travel physical right now and what they are charging generally for re-cycled air–*

*I'm on the streets now.*

*What on earth for? Farnwood! He says he's on the street! ... Your father asks where?*

*One hundred yards north of my house.*

*One hundred? What are you breathing? Who is the supplier over there at the moment, Farnwood?*

*Mother, it doesn't matter. I can afford the air. Street danger is exaggerated as far as I can see–*

*Haven't you done enough? Do you realise how you have damaged us?*

*Well, I wouldn't know. The file of the incident is unavailable to me until I get home, due to–*

*Your father thinks that you won't have had that memory retained under the restrictions of your life cover.*

*That's what I was about to communicate.*

Daniel didn't notice the man until he bumped into him. The stranger shoved a piece of paper into his hand and moved on. Daniel's I-Kno alarmed because it couldn't ID him. He turned to watch the small figure hurry away, unable to tell what colour he was: brown maybe, or copper.

*I suppose, on the plus side, we were very lucky that the safety field on the escalator was faulty, because of the settlement we received. Your father was wise to spend the extra on those insurance policies for you, but this cannot happen again, is that understood?*

Daniel unfolded the piece of paper carefully. He looked around. The street was empty. *I'll see you soon,* he thought distractedly and disconnected. He read the handwritten note:

*Stop the suicide attempts. You're attracting attention. They will be suspicious of the memory folds. I'm working on a solution. Meet soon.*

*Yours, a friend.*

Memory folds? Gene-Mart had mentioned them hadn't she? Daniel fingered the small pouch at the bottom of the page, feeling the shape of the two small pumps inside. There was a tiny scrawl indicating when to administer them. Who was the stranger? An employee? Or a trick set by his parents? When had all this started? The questions spun away from him before he could think of answers and then gave birth to more. He put his head between his hands. The Harmoniser kicked in and his breathing eased a little. In the haze of cloud above him, weather copters buzzed erratically, like Hunneybeez nearing the end of battery life. After a few moments consideration, he emptied one of the pumps into the crook of his elbow.

The house brightened slightly as he entered and after a few moments interpreting his mood, it began to adjust. The great, open floor space sprouted tiny green tongues of grass. Virtual walls appeared in unfathomable positions and gentle curving angles. Some flushed into a soft tangerine glow while others fell into mocha and biscuit. A subtle infrasonic beat pulsed through him to the strains of a beautifully played oboe. He flicked off his shoes, sat down, opened a carton of hot saké-food and closed his eyes as the grass grew between his toes. His housemate, Natalie, drifted out from the one dark corner of the large room. She was singing 'Lives of our days'. She wore only a translucent, white, linen smock. Daniel opened one eye at her voice and watched, enraptured, as she poured out her heart to him.

*How have you been? Nothing changes back here. And days are filling with tears, when I am here without you.*

*I wonder if I am a spy of some sort,* he thought.

The music stopped. *Why do you wonder this?* Natalie asked.

*Sorry, I was thinking uncensored.*

*I'm your best friend. If you can't tell me then …* She opened her arms like crucifixion and he wanted her again.

*They said I had memory folds previously.*

Natalie began pacing up and down casually, arms behind her back. She switched back to oral. "Somex: memory-hiding drug allegedly used in high espionage. Two administrations are required: the first immediately after the event one wishes to hide; the second, at a later date, acts as a catalyst for the first, by degrading the real memory and folding a fake one over it, thus hiding it, even from the subject themselves."

"Yes, something like that."

Natalie stopped and licked her heavy lips. "Do you have something to tell me Daniel?" She squatted in front of him, dewy-eyed with concern. "This is not helping our relationship. You seem to have a lot of censored thoughts at the moment."

"I know and I want to make it up to you. Like you say: *quid pro quo.*" It was Natalie's favourite saying. "I'll buy that African vacation you've been recommending."

"You won't regret it, Daniel; it's incredibly authentic, just as it would have been fifty years ago. I'll book it immediately."

Daniel smiled. Every time he ordered an experience of or above a certain value, he got a voucher towards a session with one of the Natalie clones. He had accumulated eighteen vouchers during the past two years, but was still twelve short of the target. For fifteen he could have a day with Jennifer Lopez or a week with Orlando Bloom, but as yet he had resisted the temptation. Daniel reached out to his housemate's face and his hand passed right through it.

"What is all this spy nonsense about?" she asked.

Daniel stood up. *May I have selfish minutes please?*

Natalie looked hurt, as she always did at what had recently become a much more frequent request. She sang the chorus. *"I wanna see your blue eyes, hold you so tight, I'm counting every second until tonight. I want–"*

"So am I."

The music stopped again. *Then why the request for selfishness? You've just got back. I don't understand you anymore. I mean, why did you have your clones put down? The opportunities they could have taken up in your absence.*

*I didn't trust them.*

*Do you realise how ridiculous that last statement was?*

*I don't feel myself.*

*What does that mean?*

*I just want five minutes please, and then I'll tell you my secret.*

She rose like gossamer and turned away. *Okay, Daniel, you're the boss. You never let me forget that do you?* She walked back into the darkness.

Daniel scanned the archive footage of his suicide. It appeared he had taken an opportunity given to him by a faulty escalator in the foyer of The Perpetual Evening Retirement Home: the building in which his grandfather rested. The CCTV images were from a distance. They showed the escalator stopping and the people on it waiting for assistance. A few moments later, a figure, just discernibly Daniel, could be seen climbing over to test that the safety field had also failed and then freefalling 100 feet to the foyer floor. In a stroke of luck, the voiceover said, the man landed feet first and there had been minimal damage to his brain, leaving investigating officers with vital recent memories, which would help them understand the nature of the claim.

Daniel went to the seamless curve of glass that formed the walls of his house. It had begun to rain; the weather men had been successful. He switched off the umbrella and the rain pattered noisily all around him. The organic glass absorbed it immediately, slaking the thirst of the house and leaving his view uninterrupted. He had four minutes before Natalie was back. He didn't want to tell her his secret, but he knew he would.

Some 200 yards distant, he could see his nearest neighbour's house glowing faintly through the algae-filled walls. Daniel had an idea.

*Hi, Levi, I wondered if I might be able to come over.*

*Come over?*

*Yes, I know it's unusual. I have just got out of hospital. I need someone to talk to. Ten minutes should suffice.*

*I'll come to you virtually in–*

*No, I need skintime. My doctor advised me, but I haven't had time to arrange it.*

*I don't believe that skintime stuff. You've everything you need right there, Schema.*

*I'll pay you double and I won't ask again.*

The man was quiet for a moment. *I really don't need this stress. Contact my lawyer.*

Daniel instructed his virtual lawyer to contact Levi's. An agreement was drawn up in just under two minutes: triple credit for five minutes' skintime.

Daniel injected the second pump the stranger had given him and took an unused knife from his storage container. It had already stopped raining. He paused at the perimeter of his neighbours grounds, waiting for entry. He could see Levi, his silhouette anyway, and he wondered for a moment if the man had changed his mind. Finally, the shield came down and Daniel broke into a run, wielding the knife theatrically in the air above him and screaming as he accelerated across the immaculate lawns.

"I'm going to kill you, Levi!"

There was a tiny movement as a hidden turret near the summit of the dwelling turned in his direction and he closed his eyes instinctively. A second later, a snub-nosed high-explosive shell hit him in the chest and vaporised him.

Levi turned his property's protective field back on and dashed outside. A fine, pink mist was just settling and it peppered him with tiny points of scarlet. He surveyed the mess and addressed the foot, which still stood upright in front of him, a shin bone poking like a shattered twig from the bottom of a white trouser leg.

"You're going to pay for this, neighbour."


"Good morning it is, Mr. Schema. Just confirm by opening your new eyes upon your new first day."

Daniel rubbed his eyes. "Aren't I the lucky one?"

After his physical checks and breakfast, he was summoned for an assessment.

"How are you feeling today?" Dr Gene-Mart asked, looking over her horn-rimmed glasses.

"Great! What's the point of them?" Daniel gestured at the glasses.

"Just image reinforcement; they subconsciously reassure patients of my intellectual capacity."

"Really?"

"Do you ever get tired of being so awkward, Mr Schema?"

"Yes I do actually, which is why I want to be dead."

"I'm sorry, but we are contractually obliged to keep regenerating you. Your parents are very concerned, not to mention embarrassed."

"How would you know?"

"We discussed–"

"Why would they discuss anything with a bronze?"

The doctor sighed. "It's a top policy, you really should be grateful."

"For what? Dragging me back from heaven?" He regretted the words instantly.

"Heaven was disproved twenty-five years ago, Mr Schema, thanks to what we learned from the Malaysian black butterfly. Unless *you* have something momentous to offer us after your experiences?"

Daniel glared at her.

"I didn't think so. Well, if you consent, we can alter your neuroses so that you don't want to die anymore."

"Maybe it's not where it used to be."

"Pardon?"

"Heaven. All the souls may have left it and moved on to someplace we can't find."

Gene-Mart sniggered. "Forgive me, Mr Schema. Where did you download such absurdity?"

He put his head into his hands. "I didn't; my grandfather thinks … It doesn't matter." He looked up again suddenly. "Have I changed since my first regeneration? I mean, am I still the old Daniel?"

"Of course you are. The problem of continuity of consciousness is really just a philosophical one, Mr Schema. Aren't we recreated every moment into a new moment, a new experience and a new existence?"

"I had strange thoughts in my original," he whispered.

"When?"

"The first time I disconnected. I think I lost something in regen. I think we all do."

Dr Gene-Mart sighed. "We are a little nonplussed at your behaviour. Hopefully Bioinformatics will yield some answers. We think it may be a nonsense mutation in your DNA sequence, one we haven't encountered before." She smiled. "Of course, it may be that you are simply over energising your thinking. Most people cannot afford a second chance, let alone a third. You're a Goldtint living in the age of enlightenment. Enjoy yourself."

Daniel sat up again, feeling a little dizzy. "I'd like to kill you physical," he said and was rewarded with an involuntary stiffening of the doctor's posture.

"You could pay for a clone?"

"Not a clone: you, Gene-Mart."

"Killing me would not benefit you in any way. I have a comprehensive policy and after regeneration I would be authorised to have you transplanted" – She pointed a beautifully lacquered finger at his head – "into an animal of my choice."

They stared at each other for a moment. He knew she was scared despite her display of calm. Pain was pain after all and she couldn't be sure the room would bring him down in time if he did decide to move on her. It was all there in her eyes, for just a second. Daniel leaned forward and she flinched. "My policy provides for five regenerations I understand."

"That is correct."

"Then I need only have this conversation three more times."

Dr Gene-Mart switched off her file and stood up. "Have a nice day, Mr Schema."

"As short as I can make it."

She left him with the pre-life tutorial burning his retinas. It was another three days before they allowed him to leave.

He had forgotten all about the giraffe.

"Bugger!" he shouted as his house went into operation. "How long have you been waiting?"

There was a brief pause in which he could see something in the animal's tiny eyes, searching for an appropriate answer.

"Thirteen weekth," it slobbered.

"I say, you've got a terrible lisp there."

"What ith a lithp?"

"Never mind. Let's have a look at your room." He followed the ungainly animal through to a room that reeked of coconut. Daniel surveyed the new room for a few moments. It was filled with dwarf acacias and equipped with a cleansing hole to suck away the animal's scented waste.

"You have opened your bowels it seems."

"What ith—?"

"Forget it. Acacia trees sweet enough for you?"

"Yeth, very nith."

"Well, watch those thorns, they look dreadfully sharp."

Natalie was waiting for him in the living area. She didn't sing for him.

"I have booked the vacation for this Wednesday. Please make sure you are here for it. I now have other offers I think would suit you." She was still bristling from their previous encounter. She spoke curtly, her South African accent heavier than usual. It made her even more attractive.

"Why do you never ask me about how I feel, about why I keep—?"

"That is not within my remit, Daniel. You know that."

"Do you really love me?"

108

Natalie's face softened. "Of course. Why else would I be here?"

Daniel downloaded the recording of his latest demise and watched it a dozen times. He found it quite funny. His parents would not, however. This time, apart from the damage to their Brandname, he had also cost them credit rather than made some. He spent an hour in his sexroom, which had received a scheduled upgrade while he had been away. He used some of the sex experience he had negotiated with Nurse Amber. Full immersion virtuality allowed him to relive one of her sexploits through the retinas of a bull of a man, Nordic-looking, who had got too emotionally involved and done some un-negotiated damage to one of her clones. It was simultaneously quite exhilarating and depressing. He wanted the real Natalie, wanted to treat her better than that.

Natalie tried to sell him a sample from the new range of Screen Idols when he came back. It was poor timing. The advertisement jumped into sharp focus in the centre of his living space. His nose was filled with aromas of bergamot and orange blossom as the idols sauntered towards him holding hands. They were the Classics Stable: Monica Bellucci, George Clooney, Clive Owen and Angelina Jolie; fifteen vouchers or five hundred thousand dollars a night and twenty thousand for the pre-teen range. He looked across at his housemate, who was standing, hands on hips, watching him intently. The giraffe had joined them.

"I don't want this," he protested.

Natalie pointed for him to continue watching. George Clooney asked Daniel some intimate questions and he was not forthcoming. It faded out early after a few more torturous minutes.

"How embarrassing," Natalie said.

"I don't want Hollywood clones."

"Why?"

"I want you."

"You have me, Daniel."

"I want a family."

"With me? That's out of your price range and unethical besides. Miss Gallo, I mean *I* … never had children. I was murdered, remember?"

"I know … It's authentically sad."

Natalie shrugged. She was everything he had ever wanted in a woman, chosen by the housing developer after they had recorded Daniel's reactions to a million stimuli. He was not alone in that regard. She was the most popular female housemate in the country, had been for close on three seasons, since she had been classified as the most beautiful woman ever by Time Home Management. It wasn't fair; Daniel had always had a Natalie, even when there had been such a craze on Emmanuelle Béart two years ago. One hundred and twenty million other people having Natalie as their housemate somehow made her slightly less attractive. Just recently, Daniel had found himself wondering if the original Gallo had been different to the twenty clones now under licence. Now, he had an overwhelming urge to get away from her for a while. He decided to visit his grandfather. While he waited for a cab, he ordered some mountain air for his neighbour, Levi: an apology for dying on the man's property.

Within half an hour he was at The Perpetual Evening Retirement Home. A porter led him down a long, grey corridor of closed doors. The whole building seemed to be made up of corridors. Finally, the porter stopped at a door and ushered him in.

The sky was cloudless. Daniel carefully made his way down into the steep-sided quarry, avoiding spreads of moss and occasional tufts of wild grass. Here and there, the roots of dead trees hung out of the chalk. He shaded his eyes with his hand as he looked across the deep, still pond that lay a few yards in front of him. His grandfather sat on the other side on an old wicker basket, a fishing rod perched on two rests beside him. Daniel waved. The old man gave an almost imperceptible nod and Daniel made his way over.

"Hi, Grandfather. How are you?"

"Grandfather? I told you before, don't come down here spouting that bullshit to me."

Daniel adjusted his teller to match the old man's vernacular.

"Sorry, Gramps. How are you?"

"Dead, and you?"

"I'm fine. You're hardly dead, Gramps."

"Oh yes, I'm retired aren't I?"

They always started with this. His grandfather needed to get it all off his chest before they could speak of anything else.

"I voted for another regeneration, you know that?"

"I also know your parents outvoted you and had me retired after two regens – as soon as they could do so by law in other words. Yet your dad's had six and that bitch he married must be into double figures."

"Eight this June."

Daniel watched the tip of the float slide away into the dark water. The old man, who had been holding his hands over the rod like a jaded gunslinger at his holsters, now lifted the rod swiftly and the tip of it began to quiver. A dirty, green tench was soon in his hands. He unhooked it and flung it on the dirt beside his basket, where it flapped listlessly.

"Aren't you going to put it back?"

"Why?" the old man laughed.

"I don't know. It seems cruel is all."

He watched the fish's glistening sides began to matt as it flipped and gasped in the dust.

"Eight? That is a goddamn disgrace. How do they bypass the law like that?"

"With a special dispensation because of the company's contributions to society."

"Ha! Special dispensation my ass! That's always been a euphemism for a big fat bribe. I started that company, ran it when it was respectable. Now it's just a way of making people want whatever shit you happen to be peddling this season."

Daniel couldn't remember if his grandfather had been this cantankerous before retirement. Maybe, but he wasn't supposed to be now, not according to his retirement policy. It was a good thing Daniel's mother never visited her father-in-law; she would have certainly had some alterations made. Of course he had never been a lovable old curmudgeon either, more a ruthless businessman, but the stereotype in the program was agreeable to Daniel.

The old man hooked another maggot and flung the line across the water. Daniel sat down on the chair next to him. It was the only other physical object in the room.

"Can I ask you something?"

"Yep!" he never took his eyes off the water.

"What was it like before?"

"Before what?"

"The Neural Web."

"I don't know, quieter I guess."

"Is that all?"

"Pretty much." He gave Daniel a quizzical look and smiled. "I bet you've got a hundred people badgering you right now haven't you?"

The wind got up a little, pulling the line out across the water. The old man turned the reel and tightened the line.

"Aggie was here again."

Daniel thought about the attempt the retirement home had made at recreating his grandma from the family's memories. It had been a complete disaster. "Gramma died before this new procedure came along. You know that?"

"Well, I see her out the corner of my eye sometimes, just wandering around … She cries a lot."

"How can she be here?"

"I'm guessing she has nowhere else to go."

After a while, he stood and reeled his line in. "Come on; we'll try under the willows. I reckon they'll be headed for the shade now."

Daniel folded his chair. His grandfather went ahead with the basket on his back and the rod in his hand, planting his feet carefully on the uneven ground as he made his way around the pond. Daniel flicked sweat away from his forehead as he walked. They sat in the shade of the willow trees for an hour, but didn't get another bite.

"I might not be back to see you again," Daniel said.

"Found a way out?"

"I think so."

"Where are you going, son?"

Daniel knew that what stood in front of him at that moment was merely a free-thinking composite programme based upon everything that was ever recorded of his grandfather, but occasionally it felt like something more.

"I don't know, Gramps. Heaven I hope."

The representation smiled grimly. "I think you already tried that. The last time I saw Aggie around here, you were with her."

An envelope was waiting for Daniel back at reception. A message from the badly tinted man again. He read the handwritten note, but his mind was on what his grandfather had said.

"Today's the day," he said, staring at the paper. He fired the pump into his arm and hurried home, feeling a strange detachment to any action he chose now.

As he entered his house, the Biometrics warned him he was showing acute anxiety. His Harmoniser compensated, taking the edge from his panic as he went to work. He followed the precise instructions on the note. Natalie, unable to read his thoughts, became suspicious. She came out naked to see what he was up to.

*What are you doing, Daniel? Look at me. Why are you censoring?*

Daniel did not look at her, but it was so difficult. He could see the graceful lines of her body out of the corner of his eye. He stood in the centre of the room, staring at the note, his eyes blinking rapidly as he negotiated the lengthy and numerous procedures needed to turn his home off. The walls of his house darkened and a deep, tremulous music played as he thought his way through checks, queries, warnings and veiled threats from his utility suppliers.

"Stop this, please! We can be together, Daniel! I can negotiate it!" Natalie insisted, forcing a smile.

He looked into her raw, blue eyes, flashing between melancholy and mischief. "Physical," he demanded.

"Yes."

"But I still won't know what she was really like … the original I mean: the girl who wrote those songs, who died for her beliefs."

Natalie opened her arms. "That's me, Daniel."

"No, the original is unique." He clenched his fists. "You lose something when you first die, something you can't replace. I threw it all away."

"Threw what away?"

"The old me … the real me. I didn't know what I had because it was drowned out by all this shit." Daniel smacked the side of his head savagely. He went back to the note and continued its instructions. Natalie sent him some images: the two of them were in a log-built house by the edge of a wood. They were playing with a boy and a girl who looked just like them.

"You lie!" he screamed.

"Look, a family!" she sobbed. "Please, Daniel ... I love you!"

She had never said that before. He put his hand out and pointlessly tried to wipe away her tears. "The real Natalie wouldn't love me."

Twenty minutes later, he let the note fall from his trembling hand. The house was quiet and colourless. Natalie was gone; she had blinked out mid-scream some five minutes previously. For a few seconds, he simply listened to his own breathing while the sweat dripped from his nose. He called in the giraffe. The creature sat in front of him nervously.

"Would you like oral or intercourth?"

"Neither," Daniel instructed. "I want to ask you some questions."

The giraffe nodded its patchwork head.

"Many years ago, your ancestors lived freely in Africa. Do you know of this?"

The giraffe thought for a moment. "What ith Africa?"

"It's a dead country."

"What ith anthethtors?"

"Never mind. Are you happy here?"

"I am happy with you."

"You've no dignity."

"What ith dignity?"

"It's just a word I guess."

There was a knock at the door.

"Somebody's knocking at my door. Isn't that quaint, Miss Giraffe? I just thought ... Do you have a name? Am I supposed to name you?"

"My name ith–"

"Doesn't matter! Come in, come in, whoever you are!"

A man came into the house and paused in the living room doorway. He admired the giraffe. "I've always wanted a Cleverpet."

Daniel recognised the man who had given him the note in the street. "Who are you?"

"Mr Link. You were led to me a year ago through some intermediaries. You asked me to arrange a permanent."

Mr Link slid into the room, stopping by the giraffe to pat its head. The animal turned away from his attentions.

"Guess what? I'm just going to believe you. The police will be here in about half an hour because I've closed my home down. What can you do?"

"It's already done. I adulterated your DNA today and wiped your consciousness file."

"You did?"

"Yes, Mr Schema."

Daniel scanned the man's variegated face. He was a Coppertint but it hadn't taken very well. "How did you manage to do that, then?"

"I work as a low-tech engineer at the hospital. I know where they store the DNA strands and the consciousness files."

Daniel laughed. "That's all very well, but the security is unbreakable."

"I've spent a year drifting it."

Daniel had heard of drifting of course: a rare skill that was thought to be caused by the effects of modern networking upon the brain. It was said that a drifter could send his psyche through solids for sometimes up to an hour if undisturbed.

"I thought drifting was an urban myth."

"They'd like you to believe that." Mr Link glanced at the fitful glow in the walls of the house. "We have fifteen minutes now before the squads arrive. I *must* leave here in five."

Daniel made a decision. "You want credit I presume?"

"I believe you have level two?"

"Yes and I'm willing it to you now." Daniel had received a steady drip of concerned messages, offers of advice and legal threats since he turned his home off and all but disconnected from the web. Now he attempted to think in his code against the tide.

Mr Link spent the next minute pacing up and down in agitation. "Come on! Come on!"

"They're performing security checks. How did you get into the hospital archives anyway? Drifting is one thing, but you still have to physically get in there."

Mr Link stopped pacing and gave a shaky grin. "I told you, I work there, and through drifting I pinpointed certain moments of slackness in security. It is seconds we are talking about, but if you know which seconds ..." He wandered over to the giraffe and ran his hands down its neck and then back up against the nap of the animal's fur. He twisted the giraffe's face and kissed it. "This is a very nice animal. Do you want to come with me, baby?"

The giraffe sat down heavily and shook its head. Mr Link turned away. "I'd make you if I had more time. Is it done yet?"

"It's done." Daniel felt like he should say something more profound but nothing came to mind.

Mr Link pulled a gun from his jacket and placed it against Daniel's forehead. It was warm and hard. Daniel realised that the dull throb in his throat must be fear. He closed his eyes and waited for the silence.

The squads arrived eight minutes late due to a violent electrical storm which stalled their cars. The house was dark and quiet. They found Daniel Schema on the floor of his living space with half of his head missing. A small giraffe was attempting to undo his trousers with its teeth. The attending officer drew his weapon and pointed it at the beast.

"Tell us everything you know," he ordered.

"Good morning, it is Mr Schema. Just confirm by opening your new eyes on your new first day."

Daniel sat up slowly. "How?" he asked in a whisper.

Nobody answered. There was just the babbling room trying to mollify him, while its sterility, its stark light, scratched his new eyes like nano-thin razorblades. He curled up on the bed with his head pressed against his knees and rocked back and forth slowly.

Breakfast came: green algae on toast, mango juice and a sweet green tea. As Amber placed it on the table, Daniel leapt to his feet and the girl just made it to the door. Her yelp of fear encouraged him. He threw the tray and they brought him down with an infrasonic pulse. When he woke, there was a new tray on the table and a new breakfast.

"Good morning, Mr Daniel ..."

He took the tray and dashed it across the wall. They knocked him out six times before he calmed down.

"What have you done, you bitch?"

Dr Gene-Mart smiled. "What we are asked to do under provision of your insurance policy."

"But–"

"Your parents added something else. I guess you never bothered to listen to the whisperprint."

He shook his head in disbelief. His hands went up to his face and began to explore it. They probed nostrils that were wider than expected, pulled at a fuller lip, a higher cheekbone. He noticed a gleam of pleasure in Dr Gene-Mart's eyes. Finally, his hand went to the mirror. He looked in silence upon his new face.

"Mr Link kept his side of your little deal. Your DNA was not backed up I'm afraid, but your consciousness was. It's kept separately in a secure vault. So here you are in a new body."

He watched her lips in fascination, stunned by the words that were now spilling from them.

"You may develop some disparities in personality traits,

but rest assured it is a healthy donor clone. There will always be some impact between the clone body's cells and your consciousness. Cells have memories, too, and you may find you acquire a liking for things you never did before. Naturally, the donor's history will be made available to you. That's the best we can do under the circumstances, Daniel. We are not Gods." She allowed herself a smile.

Daniel realised he had smashed the mirror. "You caught him?"

"Yes, Daniel. He had been under surveillance for some time. You're going to hurt yourself with that–"

"When?"

"A few hours after he shot you I believe. He'll be in the body of a walrus by now. You know what they do to murderers, Daniel."

He was on her in an instant and the broken shard of mirror rose and fell in a rapid blur, tossing strings of bright red baubles high above him. He marvelled at their sparkle and warm patter as they fell back upon the doctor's bronze skin.

"Die, die, die!" he commanded and then fell onto the dead woman as the room's control mechanism fired a lethal sonic wave through him.


The elegant, high-ceilinged room rang with the tinkle of polite laughter. The walls were a deep, lush green. From them grew a proliferation of orchids. Their heavy petals hung in cream, damson and fiery orange, like ranks of flamboyant spectators to the party in the centre of the room. It was very warm.

A tall, platinum-tinted woman of indeterminable age was holding court to a group of eight women and four men.

"I can't thank you enough of course, Miss Gene-Mart-Schema. That has a nice ring to it, does it not?"

The tiny, Silvertinted young woman beside her nodded coyly. "You have been very generous with your patronage. I'm glad I could help. It must have been a testing time for your family."

"Indeed, but your sacrifice has helped us and Daniel greatly. I see our tinting division did an excellent job. Silver suits you."

"I'm very happy with it."

"Good. There's nothing that dents the confidence quite like a poorly applied tint."

The older woman closed her eyes for a moment. Her naked body, which was translucent due to the very latest skin fashion, began to quiver a little. The profusion of green buds that grew on her head in place of hair began to flower. In a matter of seconds, there were tiny, gold blooms covering her scalp.

"Oh, bravo, dear! Bravo!" Her husband, dressed in nothing but rolling, ten-minute skin adverts for Schema International, stepped forward to congratulate his wife. The rest of the party clapped enthusiastically as the woman beamed her delight.

"Are they gold? Are they gold?"

"Yes, Mrs Schema; a wonderful show."

One of the other women gestured at the gurgling fluids just visible inside Mrs Schema's belly. "I see you're pregnant again Mrs Schema. Congratulations."

She blushed intentionally. "The termination is in September. I like to have one every fall. It's the season for loss, don't you think?"

"Yes, indeed."

"Okay, let's see if he will grace us then."

She moved to the far side of the room with her husband as the guests took their drinks and sat at the horseshoe-shaped seating system, which faced the door. She pleaded for almost five minutes and her smile never faltered.

"Be a good boy, now. All these people are here to see you on your birthday. Occasionally, she adjusted her teller to see if that would work. "Cum in heah dis minnit!" she demanded and then softening again, "I membahs de time wen you wah jus a chile, you neva dis bad. C'mon honey, fer ya mammy."

One of the seated parties called through. "Is that Slave?"

The woman re-adjusted her teller and turned her head.

"Yes, do you like it? Farnwood thinks it's too gauche."

Finally, the lion stretched lazily into a standing position and padded out of the den past the man and woman. In the living room there were a number of people the creature recognised. They all looked at him expectantly. He had been taught to sing a birthday song at this moment but he didn't want to. He moved into the centre of the room, opened his enormous mouth and yawned. The seated people shuffled a little and sipped their drinks. The young Silvertinted woman stood up shakily. "Hi, how are you doing today?"

The lion studied her with pale, yellow eyes. His lolling sandpaper tongue probed the empty gums in his mouth. His thick paws attempted to unsheathe claws long since removed.

The naked man flashed a brilliant white smile at him. "Come on, son. Friends and family are all here and we have a birthday surprise. Here she is, in person."

At his words, there came the sound of a guitar being strummed and out of a side door, Natalie Gallo appeared, swinging her guitar as she sang, "*I once knew a man brought back to life …*"

She wore loose cargo pants, a blue T-shirt with a golden dragon writhing on it and over that, a blue, unzipped hoodie. Her hair was cut short, but the fringe was long, whipping across her face as she moved.

"*You might be that man I adored. But you don't seem to remember, how we met and what your heart ached for.*"

The lion pawed at the floor and roared. The eight seated people jumped to their feet and backed away. There was some whimpering. Miss Gallo stopped singing abruptly and looked at Mrs Schema in terror.

The woman waved impatiently. "Continue, continue! He can't harm you – no cock or claws."

The guitar started up again tentatively. *"I'm … I'm all out of faith and I'm waiting in heaven … now it's empty without you …"* Natalie Gallo's nostrils flared with emotion as she opened her voice for the climax of the song and her haunted eyes never left the lion's face. After the applause, there was an awkward silence. Miss Gallo turned to the Schemas.

"Was it okay, then?"

Mr Schema smiled. "Well, son, what did you think of that?"

The lion squatted over the grass carpet and its face contorted with effort. The smell of lavender filled the room.

★ ★ ★

… Moises looked around at Dollie and the man jumped a little, surprised by the boy's movement.

"Why have you quit?"

"Water," Moises croaked.

Isaacs handed him a bottle, which he downed in two long draughts.

Dollie leaned forward. "Did you feel me shaking you earlier?"

"No."

"Appears you can't be reached when you're in the thick of it."

Moises yawned long and hard. He was feeling lightheaded and hungry. The stories were getting harder for him to take. That last one … well, the sickness of it hung on him.

The Texan also seemed to be struggling with something; his mouth moved silently as he looked at some notes he had made. "You tired, boy?" he asked, looking up from his pad.

It was hard to concentrate on Dollie's words. "Yes, very tired now."

Dollie sighed. "Well, we got a ways to go yet. What do you think of these stories, Moises?"

"They seem … true."

Dollie looked him with a kind of awe.

"I think you're right … Hell, I know you are somehow."

Moises shrugged. "*Me perecen íntimos.*"

"They are." The flat voice came from the shadows across the room. Moises turned and peered at them, trying to pick out the speaker. It was a voice he did not recognise. There was a strangeness to it, an accent of some sort.

"What do you mean, Wendell?" Dollie asked, and the man stepped out from the shadows. He was slightly overweight, short-haired, pale and plain-looking; the jeans, sneakers and light jacket, wholly inappropriate for the situation, marked him out as a foreigner, newly arrived in Peru.

"From what we know about Hawthorne, this boy's obsession with the pop star, and some of the other elements in the stories" – The man pointed at Moises – "a percentage of this is coming from him. I am not sure why though … or how much."

"Holy Mary and Joseph!" Dollie whispered. "I make you right."

Moises stared at the man and Dollie answered the unspoken question. "Wendell here is a bit of an expert on esoterica. I brought him in from Germany a bit back."

For a few moments, Dollie and Wendell moved away and discussed something in whispers. Dollie turned back to Moises.

"Just get back to it, now."

Moises shook his head. "I want to sleep for a bit."

Dollie's shadow fell over him. "You want to join your family right now, is that it?"

Moises shook his head wearily, but a growing part of him longed for what the Texan was threatening. He wanted to be away from this place so badly, far away, with his brother Mayta perhaps, drinking ice cold beers not in Iquitos, but in that English pub Hawthorne often talked about … that Moat House. And yet, Mayta was even further away than England wasn't he? In a country of the dead that Moises could not imagine. Still, it was a nice dream to have and he could see it as clearly as the room around him, more clearly even.

"What are you grinning at?" Asked Dollie.

Moises ignored him and turned back to the table. He looked down the microscope, cleared his throat and felt his eyes drawn to an unfurling story once again …

# THIS SIDE OF THE OTHER SIDE

I sit outside for a while, nervously dipping my fingers in lager, and tracing around the tropical fish on the cover of the album I always bring along. It's a still, hot day and the manager comes out in a lilac shirt to raise the parasols. I nod at him, squinting at the sun bouncing back off the white washed walls of the old building.

"You're early today Chris, got a day off?"

"Yes ... it's Sean's birthday."

He smiles sympathetically. "Is it? How are your mum and dad keeping?"

"Not bad thanks."

Steve picks an empty crisp packet off the bench and scrunches it in his fist. "Didn't they fancy coming down?"

"No, it upsets them too much nowadays ... you know?"

Steve nods. "Hope it goes well." He slaps me on the shoulder and moves along. I turn away from the blinding walls. From where I am sitting I can watch people coming into the pub. There is a shallow moat around the building, and a small stone bridge out front is the only way across from the car park. A young couple cross the bridge and sit at the bench opposite me. The man parks the baby carriage so it is under the parasol, then sets the brakes on the wheels and goes into the pub. The woman tears open a packet of crackers. She passes one to the tiny outstretched hand in front of her and licks her fingers. She is very attractive. I take a gulp of lager and try not to watch her cooing at her baby. I fail.

A family pull up in a people carrier and walk slowly across the bridge. They pause to look into the moat, pointing animatedly at any fish they see. The water is flat and dusty in the midday heat. I watch it now, to see if I can spot what is exciting them. After a few moments the thick, pale lips of a large carp break the surface. There is a prolonged slurp, and the water curls as the fish turns away. The pretty woman makes a little gasp and looks embarrassed at having done so. "Wow, what was that?" she asks, thinking out loud.

"A carp," I say, mesmerised by how clear and blue her eyes are.

She opens them wider. "Big fish aren't they?

"Yes," I confirm, they are. She goes back to cooing at her child.

I want to tell her that my brother and I caught those fish fourteen years ago, from a lake almost thirty miles from here. I want to describe how Sean used to fill a holdall up with water, and how he would sit in the back of the car with the carp, bream, or whatever it happened to be that day, stroking the fish to comfort them as they were transported to a new home. Every fish in that moat was brought here lovingly, illegally, by my brother Sean. Nobody knows that. Why should they? It isn't important to them.

I don't tell her anything of course. Her husband comes back with a pint and a half and gives me a quick look that might be a warning.

One of the barmaids appears with a ticket in her hand.

"Chris Dallán?"

"Yes."

"Your contact is available now."

I grab my album and follow the girl inside. I hear a familiar voice and see a grin appear out of the gloom. It's Turtle. "Alright Chris, you look lost?"

"Bloody sun, I've gone blind walking in here."

Turtle was one of my brother's old friends. Ribs, Donn and Jimmy are sitting with him. We exchange a bit of forced banter, but it's still nice to see them. Ribs stands up - there isn't a great deal of change in his height - and pushes his hand through his black wavy hair. I've always thought he looks like Johnny Cash in heavier gravity.

"What are you drinking?" He asks me.

Donn grabs the man's arm. "I think Chris is going for a tickle Ribs."

The other lads look at each other and smile at the inadvertent joke.

"Oh sorry, give him our best won't you?" Ribs says solemnly. "Sure."

The barmaid has been waiting for me to follow.

"I'll see you afterwards lads okay?"

They wish me luck and I follow the girl into what used to be the old restaurant. She ushers me in and closes the door behind me. I've always liked the feel of the room since the pub got its contact licence; it holds an atmosphere that is heavy with feeling but not oppressively so. The walls are cushioned in purple velvet, lined with black butterfly prints, and the glass chandeliers throw intricate shapes across its nap. The room has been extended out back. There are ten lanes - curtained off from one another - that run for about twenty feet. At the end of each is a soft armchair facing a gleaming, ceiling high mirror. It looks like a cross between a bowling alley and an up market brothel. I make my way to the bar. The barman greets me and I hand him my ticket.

"Thank you Mr. Dallán." He says, reading my name from a list. He doesn't know me; I usually come in the evenings.

"Do you have a familiar?"

"Yes," I give him my album. He carefully takes the inner sleeve and the vinyl out and hands me back the cover. "Musiquarium ... classic album," he smiles.

"Yes it is."

He taps something into his hand pad. "Your brother is receiving, is that correct?"

"I hope so."

The eerie silence is broken by something happening to my left. A young woman at the seating area appears to be upset. She is surrounded by family members, and there is a barmaid bending over her, whispering reassurances. I watch the young woman's blonde hair whip back and forth as she shakes her head violently. Words come sporadically, rising up like snatches of song from a radio station struggling for signal: "Rip off ... never would have said that ... looks nothing like him ... my money back."

"That's one hundred and fifty pounds please." The barman says.

I take out my wallet and hand over the thin slab of notes, still warm from the cash machine. Account balance: minus 3900, Account available: 100. The cold numbers are still burning in my mind. I rarely check my balance: it's better not to know. I haven't missed a call for six months but it suddenly strikes me that I won't be able to afford it next week. The thought is unbearable.

The barman turns to the glass counter behind him which is bathed in soft spotlights, and presses a small shot glass up to the only optic on the wall. The bottle squirts a measure of limpid, violet liquid: the feather, or the tickle; it's the substance that connects worlds, if you believe in all that, and I do.

"Lane seven, here's your feather sir." He puts the glass on the counter and nods at his pad. "I see you've been before."

"Yes."

"So you know to-"

"Leave it ten minutes, yes."

I take my feather and sink into an armchair. The young woman is being led out now. She is sobbing. There is an elderly couple sitting opposite, looking a little anxious. They smile politely at me. Only two of the purple curtains are drawn. I stare down lane seven and flip my feather. The drink tastes like Parma violets, which apparently isn't deliberate. Still, everything to do with this business has a purple-ness. It seems contrived to me, like the strategy of a marketing campaign.

I clutch my album cover to my chest and close my eyes. The next thing I know the barman is shaking my shoulder.

"You better go now sir, or you'll miss your connection."

I look around sleepily. The old couples have gone and all the alleys are free. It's just me now. I hurry to alley seven. The barman pulls the heavy, noise reductive curtain behind me.

The high backed armchair sits six feet from the mirror. I slip into its shadow and sink my head back. All is dim here, except for the centre of the mirror. I put my earphones on and that funky clavinet riff rises to meet me. Smiling, I whisper the fist lines of 'Superstition'. I stare into the centre of the mirror, focusing on my lips as they move through the song. The light drops a touch, as if somebody is turning a dimmer switch somewhere. That familiar feeling builds above my eyes. In my mind something delicate begins to swirl, a feather spinning as it slowly falls to a surface too far away to contemplate. I resist the urge to scratch my head: the tickle cannot be reached from this side. The mirror is clouding again and I anticipate what happens next by shutting my eyes. My ears pop. It always makes me jump, and then the mirror clears a little.

"Sean, is that you Sean?"

The man in the mirror moves away for a second and then turns back. I can smell fishing nets, and luncheon meat drying in the sun.

"What the ..?" The face looms large for a second, like someone at a peephole. It's Sean alright, but he looks shocked, visibly upset.

"Sean, what's up?"

The face looks away, I hear words disjointed. Then it turns back once again. "Oh Chris it's you ... it's really you."

"Sean I-"

"After all these years ... really?"

"It's only been a week Sean."

My brother shakes his head. "No, much longer than that."

"It's always a-"

"-week, yes I remember it used to be."

"I come every Friday night, only today I came earlier because-"

"-but then it was a month, and then nearly a year-"

"-it's your birthday."

"God, it must be fifteen years since I saw you, longer."

"I come every week Sean."

My brother looks away again and speaks to someone out of sight. Fifteen years! The last two sessions had been marred by this disparity in time between us. I had eventually just let it go; maybe Sean... maybe the dead, perceive time differently. That is what the landlord had said anyway, although he didn't seem sure. Nobody knows why this miraculous system is so suddenly falling apart. We all just persist, hoping for the best. But fifteen years; how long would it be next time? The idea paralyses my thoughts.

"Who's there with you?" I manage.

"Lynne."

"You got married?"

"Been married for twelve years. I met Lynne just after you ... well, just after your accident."

"That's great, I mean, that you can have another life over there."

Sean sighs. "Let's not start arguing over who is alive and who isn't again, not after all this time. I'm sorry bruv, but it's not my birthday either; that was three months ago, but thanks anyway."

I can feel my temples pulsing. "Oh, but you would have been forty nine today," I say weakly. Why was everything so fucking mixed up?

"I'm sixty five Chris."

"Then how come you look the same as ever?"

"Maybe because that's how you want to see me."

I can't speak for a moment. Sean is crying; nothing dramatic, just quiet water on his cheeks.

"But I come every week," I protest, and wish I could stop saying that.

Sean clears his throat. "Thanks mate, I appreciate it. I haven't stop trying either Chris, but mediums, I don't trust them, and these machines are always hit and miss. It's funny, I just had a feeling today, switched this thing on for the first time in I don't know how long, and here you are!"

I can feel how the conversation will fall into the usual pattern. I really don't want it to. But I can't stop myself.

"I'm not dead Sean."

"Look Chris-"

"I'm just saying, I really didn't die in that accident. Lost my finger though." I hold up my hand and smile.

Sean smiles back, wipes his eyes. "What a stupid thing to do; lose your finger climbing a security fence, out of your mind drunk."

"I was being chased."

"You bled to death alone."

"I … I didn't. Somebody heard me and rang an ambulance."

"I'm sorry I wasn't there Chris."

"It's okay, listen, I'm at the Moat House, it's where they do this stuff from; do you remember that? Donn's here, Ribs, Turtle … they all say hello."

"Mum and dad still alive?" Sean asks, humouring me it seems.

"At home, they send their love."

Sean puts his face in his hands, and a woman puts her arm around his shoulder. He looks up. "Are they really there? I miss you all so much."

"Yes," and suddenly I cannot stop myself. "Hey, do you remember when that old landlord Brian filled the moat with rainbow trout? We used to take our hand lines and climb over the back fence from the allotments to fish for them."

Sean laughs a little. "Of course I remember. He would often stand out front, just staring at the water. He couldn't understand where they'd all gone. It kept mum's freezer full for a couple of months."

I feel something quiver in my head, and I become aware of the chair for a second. No … no, this connection gets shorter every week! I concentrate hard, like I do when I'm waking up from a dream and I don't want to, knowing that it is futile, that I can only stall the awakening for so long. "What about when you stole that mouse I wanted, from the pet shop in town," I add quickly.

"Oh bruv, your face was a picture when I took it out of my coat on the bus. You kept asking if the Police would come for us."

I look hard at this version of my brother, trying to remember the living Sean, the man I want to see, but he is not clear in my mind.

"Pity it was pregnant. Trust me eh?" He chuckles and his

eyes light up, and it is the young Sean for a moment, before the drink got hold of him.

"How quickly did those things multiply?" I say.

"It was ridiculous. You took it pretty well when we had to dump them. You were only what ... seven?"

It goes on like this for a few minutes, batting memories back and forth like retired tennis pros playing safe shots for one another. Six months since our first contact, and it still runs the same way; the arguments, then the reminiscing, then the awkward goodbyes. I can feel the pressure building in my ears and I panic. "Sean, I'm glad you're happy there, that you're with Lynne and can have another life, a better one than-"

"You're breaking up bruv."

And suddenly, knowing somehow that this is my last chance, I say what I've wanted to for six months. "I'm so sorry about not being there for you that night, and all the horrible things I said to you when you were struggling ..."

"It's okay Chris, I got myself together."

"I wish you had, on this side I mean. You were always there for me when I needed you, but I let you down."

"You didn't let me down."

"I'm scared Sean, I don't think I'm going to get through to you anymore."

Sean's face looms large for the last time. "Maybe because it's time to move on now, for both of us."

I shake my head instinctively. "I'm going to try to get to you."

"Get to me, how?"

"The only way I can think of."

Sean stands up. "Chris, don't you-"

My ears pop violently and the mirror sways and draws itself back into unyielding light. Stevie is singing 'Superwoman' now which means I've had around twenty minutes. The nausea is stronger than ever. I put my banging head in my hands. "Damn it."

The curtain behind me is drawn back and a hand falls gently on my shoulder.

"Are you okay Mr. Dallán?"

I can't even raise my head at first. "No ... my brother's dead."

The lounge bar is dark and comforting. It smells ripe with beer and cigarettes. I sit in the corner with Ribs and the lads, sipping brandy and coke, thin layers of pale smoke stretching over our heads like stratus clouds. We feed them with our fags.

"Are you okay mate?" asks Donn, his high forehead creased in concern. They've been buying me drinks since I returned.

"A bit better now cheers. It gets harder every time. That stuff hardly works at all anymore."

Turtle drags a beer mat to the edge of the table and flicks it with the back of his hand, fails to catch it. He picks it up and tries again. "They reckon the pub might lose its licence, not enough people contacting anymore."

Jimmy speaks now, for the first time since I came back. "People are sick of paying good money for a lot of upset." Jimmy gave up contacting his mum three months ago, because she told him he didn't look like her son.

"They reckon it has all been a big con from day one, that the feather is a hallucinogenic or whatever," adds Ribs.

"Shut up Ribs you idiot," Donn kicks him under the table.

"All right, sorry." Ribs rubs his leg and looks me in the eye. "I didn't say that Chris, it's just a rumour I heard?"

"It's fine mate."

For a few moments there is just the clink of glasses being taken out of the dishwasher behind the bar.

"I don't know who is deader ... me or Sean?" The words come out because they have to, and the fact that this is not how we talk here, or anywhere else for that matter, causes an embarrassed silence.

Then Jimmy says. "What do you mean Chris?"

"Sean say's that *I'm* dead ... not him."

Jimmy laughs uneasily. "They all say that though don't they?"

"Look," says Donn, "he's confused, wherever he is. I mean, we know he's dead, I found him for Christ's sake."

I don't remember that phone call from Donn very well, just that he was crying. I'd never heard him cry before, didn't know a big man like him could cry. It was even more shocking hearing it down the phone. I felt angry at him for doing that. Sean was *my* brother after all.

He had been missing for six days, and I had been very blasé about it all. His alcoholism had become just an irritation to me in the end, something that was impossible to change. 'He'll turn up' I told my mum, 'you know what he's like'. I've worked out some excuses for the way I reacted that week. Some days I believe them. Yet I can't help coming to the conclusion that I just didn't care enough, and that is too terrible to consider.

Donn found him around the back of the pub, in the spot where we always used to go fishing. There was a bottle of cider in the grass beside him. He was lying on his back with his arms spread wide, and he was smiling.

"Here's to Sean." I raise my glass and the lads join me. They look like faded posters to me, advertising a way of life they don't really believe in anymore, and my heart fills with fondness for them.

"Maybe we're both alive somehow," I say, thinking of the rope in the garage at home, and dreaming of a more reliable connection.

"Or maybe we're both dead." I knock my drink back and ask what everybody is having.

# WENDELL'S LIST

Paul Turner felt sure that it had rained deliberately that Friday and was suitably bitter about it. He had taken an unplanned lieu day, on an urge to visit the city, and the sky had been emptying steadily since ten that morning. His day in the capital had run perfectly but despite this, the inclement weather had tainted everything for him. He stopped inside the entrance to Marylebone Station, lowered his umbrella and shook the rain from it. It was just after four and the station was busy. He didn't like crowds. On the opposite side of the station there was a small, brightly lit pub. Paul decided he would have a couple of pints while he waited for rush hour to pass.

As he put his travel card back into his wallet and thumbed through the notes inside, he sensed somebody had stopped in front of him, and looked up. A man smiled shyly and offered his hand.

"Pleased to meet you, Paul."

The man looked middle-aged. He wore red baseball shoes, washed-out jeans and a green, military-style jacket, which was very similar to Paul's. It didn't suit him because he was carrying a bit extra around the waist. His hair was shorter and a touch greyer, his nose a little straighter and there was no chickenpox scar low on his left cheek, but other than these anomalies, Paul might have been standing in front of a mirror. He registered it all in a few seconds and continued to stare. The man lowered his hand.

"You're as white as a grand wizard's washing line. Bit of a shock, huh?"

"What?" Paul asked and could think of nothing else to add. He looked around at the people hurrying across the station floor, their coats glistening with rain under the stark, orange lighting, eyes set on some personal imperative. No one gave the two men more than a glance.

"Are you a relative?"

The man smiled. "Well, you might say I am. Can I explain?"

"I wish you would."

The man put down the large, khaki holdall he was holding and flexed his hands for a moment. "I'm Wendell Perkins, out of Beatrice, Nebraska." He pronounced it Be-*at*-riss, Nuh-*bras*-ka. "I search for … well, I search for myself; there's no other way of putting it really." He looked down as colour suddenly spread across his cheekbones. "The thing is, you were on my list, so here I am."

Paul watched the man's face, every subtle movement familiar. "What list?"

"I've found a lot more."

They sat at a cold, steel table outside a café near the entrance to the Underground. Paul had suggested the pub but Wendell insisted on buying them cappuccinos. Paul thought it made them look gay. A few awkward moments were passed, blowing and sipping at their coffees.

"I see you're an artist like the rest of us," the American gestured at 'The Sunflowers' umbrella Paul had bought at the National Gallery. The twenty pound price tag was still gnawing at him.

"I dabble."

"I saw you at the London Gallery–"

"The National Gallery."

"Whatever! You're interested in art, so I figure you like to paint … I mean, we all do."

"You've been following me? Who's we?"

Wendell banged his coffee cup down on the table and it spilled across his hand. He winced and shook his steaming hand. "I'm sorry, but I have a procedure," he said sharply. "I like to make sure I've got the right person."

"Well, I don't like being stalked." Paul was past shock and had quickly moved onto embarrassment, then anger at the manner in which he had been approached.

Wendell looked up at the steel buttressing high above them and raised his voice. "I show him a miracle and all he does is bellyache," he said, but the words seemed to stall under the cavernous roof. He checked his watch as if he now wanted to be away.

"We're look-a-likes, so what?" Paul asked.

"We're much more than that."

"Really? Is that why you've copied what I'm wearing? In fact, how did you even know what I was wearing today?"

"Please, let me explain." Wendell unzipped the bulging holdall at his feet. He pulled forth a ring binder and his face cleared suddenly. He set the binder on the silver-hatched table top and flipped it open. "Are you in a hurry?"

"Listen, if this is some kind of con, you picked the wrong man. I'm not signing up to anything; I don't care how much you look like me."

Wendell smiled as he flicked the pages. "This is not a con, I promise you that." He found the page he was looking for and brought out a camera. "You don't mind, do you?"

The flash seared Paul's eyes.

"Could you fill out this questionnaire for me?"

"I don't think so."

"Please, it will only take five minutes and it helps to prove my theory."

"Your theory?"

"I've met lots of us, Paul, and we not only look the same, we have the same personalities."

Paul drained his coffee and frowned. "Impossible! I mean, don't they say we are products of our environment?"

"Yes and no; our lives develop in roughly the same way, despite cultural differences and demographics." Wendell spun the ring binder so it was facing Paul, clicked a Paper Mate and offered it over. The ring binder held a three-sheet, typed questionnaire, which had Paul's name printed at the top. There was a box in the top, left-hand corner, which Paul presumed was for his photograph.

"But we have different parents, therefore different genes. We can't be the same."

"You wouldn't think so, but the law of averages allows for it eventually. There have never been more people on earth than at this particular moment in time."

Paul picked up the pen and began to fill in the form. "If that's true, there would be doubles of everyone."

"Eventually maybe. In any case, the days of the individual are numbered. We are the proof that nature is finally running out of ideas."

Paul would never have admitted it, but there did appear to be more than just a physical similarity between them. He recognised Wendell's little facial tics and seemed to understand the thoughts and emotions that forced each idiosyncratic movement, whether it was a furrowing of the brow, a lick of the lips or just a slight flash in the eyes. It was all, however, completely ridiculous.

"Okay then," he smiled, "how many have you found so far?"

"You're number ten and I have a list of sixty."

"Sixty?"

"Finish the questionnaire. I need a smoke." Wendell got up and walked to the open doorway to Harewood Avenue. Paul watched the American light up a cigarette with a Zippo and blow a large cloud into the darkening street. This would be the perfect moment to leave, but Paul's curiosity was beginning to get the better of him. He finished the form.

Wendell returned and sat down. "Without looking, I'd say you were born in June or July, you are single, heterosexual, have slept with less than ten women in your entire life, possibly had at least one hernia operation and your appendix was whipped out when you were a kid."

"Er … yes, I–"

"You are non-religious, like to think of yourself as a liberal, but secretly you are more right wing. You don't broadcast that because you think it makes you less appealing to people, especially the type of women you try to impress."

"Hang on!"

"You lack confidence. You smoke, more so when you drink, which you do too much. Your boozing leads to occasional losses of temper. You have an arrest history for violent behaviour."

Paul's cheeks were glowing. For a split second, he envisaged dragging Wendell down to the floor and smashing his smug face against the concrete until it came apart. "You got me just about bang on," he conceded instead, taking a deep breath, and handed the questionnaire back.

Wendell read through it. Occasionally, he grunted in satisfaction.

Paul felt his thudding heart begin to slow down. "Can I see the others?" he asked loudly as the station announcer told of the imminent arrival of the four fifty-two from Aylesbury.

Wendell turned a few pages and spun the folder.

## *COPIES*

*~~Lucas Oppenheimer~~ =*
*~~Age 28, Bull Creek, Missouri, USA~~*
*~~—— Robert Kristopher~~ =*
*~~Age 23, Northville, Michigan, USA~~*
*~~—— Marius Szislak~~ =*
*~~Age 7, Pensacola, Florida, USA~~*
*~~—— Herbert Mills~~ =*
*~~Age 32, Carlisle, Nova Scotia, Canada~~*
*~~—— Mark Gregan~~ =*
*~~Age 22, Toronto, Ontario, Canada~~*
*~~—— Jay Grendel~~ =*
*~~Age 68, Abbotsford, British Columbia, Canada~~*
*~~—— Gerinaldo Chavez~~ =*
*~~Age 51, Cuzco, Peru~~*
*~~—— George Estebahn~~ =*
*~~Age 45, Nueva Gorgona, Panama~~*
*~~—— Agustin Ledezma~~ =*
*~~Age 36, Catamarca, Argentina~~*
*Paul Turner*
*Age 37, Reading, UK*
*Bruno Arden*
*Age 25, Cologne, Germany*
*Viggo Hattamarensen*
*Age 17, Radlek, Estonia*

Paul turned the top page and looked at Lucas Oppenheimer's picture and biography. He then flicked through all the names of those visited so far. Despite the age differences, there was no doubting the uncanny similarities. At the back of the folder there were four more sheets, twelve names on each: names from Europe, South Africa, and New Zealand …

He closed the folder and handed it back.

"Copies?"

Wendell cleared his throat. "Well … you are all copies to me."

"How did you recognise Marius? He's only seven."

"Coincidence. He won a national art competition for kids, to produce a painting that represented the American spirit, or some bullshit. I was watching Fox News and there he was … There I was. I knew it right away."

Paul reopened the folder and looked again at the photograph of the boy. The weak mouth, the eager-to-please expression; it might have been one of Paul's old school photographs.

"And now you can cross me off."

Wendell began to put his things away carefully. Paul didn't like the man one bit. It could have been the shock of seeing himself as others did that caused most of his resentment. But Paul knew he wasn't really like Wendell. He was smarter for a start, better looking as well. Travelling the world searching for people who look like you? Could it get any sadder? And yet something about all this rang true.

The American looked down at him and frowned, as if he had heard Paul's thoughts.

Paul smiled back. "Are you going?"

"I thought I might travel with you a ways if you don't mind?"

Paul shrugged and moved away through the crowd, heading for the Bakerloo Line. Wendell slipped in front of him when they joined the queue for the escalator. The steel risers fell slowly into a long, steep drop. Paul felt the warm, greasy air sticking in his throat. The ascending escalator passed by serenely, just out of touching distance. The commuters stood straight and even, and suddenly Paul saw the uniformity of their flesh. And for a moment, the idea of diversity in human beings was gone.

Replacing it was this endless line of bodies, like stamps punched from a huge sheet of flesh and wrapped in bland clothing. He leaned forward. "How long have you been doing this, Wendell?"

"I've searched image databases for ten years now. I found you on Faces Around the World."

"But I didn't put my picture on–"

"There are cameras everywhere, Paul. You can't control where your image might turn up."

As they stepped off the escalator, a warm breeze funnelled up from the tracks, bringing an iron smell from the darkness. The crowd shuffled forward.

"You just wade through thousands of images?"

"Millions I suppose."

It was warmer still on the platform. The air was flat and empty. The crowd, like a blind organism, pushed as far as it sensed was possible and then settled, its components waiting, armless and silent in their discomfort. Paul Turner and Wendell Perkins were 10 feet away from the platform edge, although they could not see it. The opposite wall curled over to them, adorned with giant, peeling advertisements.

"Mama Mia. Its sixth sell-out year," Paul read without interest, trying to take his mind off his claustrophobia. The matrix sign above them rolled. The next train was due in one minute.

"I'd like to contact the others. Could you give me their details?"

The drone of an approaching train and a stiff breeze passed through the crowd. The train squealed to a halt in front of them. The doors slid open and there was a polite but determined surge. They might just have squeezed on but Wendell held back at the last moment.

*Beepbeepbeepbeepbeepbeepbeepbeepbeepbeepbeep!* ... *Please mind the gap!*

The doors rattled shut and the train pulled away with a rising hum. Paul could feel panic bubbling inside him.

"Where will you go from here? Germany?"

"Jeez, Paul! You ask a lot of questions you already know the answers to."

Wendell stepped back from the edge of the platform and squeezed his holdall behind Paul's legs. Paul looked down at the painted yellow line that ran 2 inches inside the lip of the concrete. The tips of his Converse trainers were touching it. He tried to shuffle back a little but there was the bag and a growing number of people pushing onto the platform. The weight of them was starting to nudge him forward and he had to keep adjusting his feet to compensate. The red dots rolled on the sign: two minutes.

Paul thought about the names on the list, scored through so carefully with a rule.

"Creationism or Evolution? Which way do you see it?" Wendell asked.

"What? Evolution I suppose."

"Of course you do. Yet lots of rational people believe in Creationism, even if it is ridiculous. Because if we came from nowhere and we go to nowhere, if we are just a stupid, improbable accident, what's the point of it all?"

"I don't know."

Wendell looked utterly miserable. "We're not even unique accidents."

Paul glanced at the matrix sign: one minute left. He felt Wendell's hands come up against his shoulders. They were shaking. From the tunnel came the clatter of an approaching train. It sounded to Paul like some giant, chittering beetle, scuttling up from a place deep in the bedrock of the planet. He imagined its antennae bristling, tasting the darkness as it moved.

145

They were about 30 feet away from the tunnel entrance. Paul stared at the tracks below him, wondering which one was live. The middle one? Or was it all of them? His thoughts dropped away, shrivelling like leaves facing an early winter. He tottered for a second as the crowd pushed harder against him, ready to fight for a spot on the approaching train. The train's headlights blinded him and he heard Wendell's words despite the roar.

"I'll feel better when none of you copies are around anymore."

With an almighty effort, Paul locked his knees and jumped back into Wendell as the man pushed him forward. They wrestled each other and screamed, like a madman staring into a funfair mirror, spinning, falling, and then one of them was snatched away so completely that the other felt the nails tear from his fingertips. Something enormous struck his legs and they caught fire with an unbearable pain. He felt the flames gutter up through his stomach and he curled like a glowing, delicate ember then went out.


It was just after midday on a cool, spring afternoon when Bruno Arden opened his apartment door to an older, slightly heavier version of him.

"*Mein Gott!* I didn't know if you would come," he said quietly.

The visitor extended his hand. "Good to finally meet you. I am—"

"Me with different memories."

"Couldn't have put it better myself."

Bruno looked around outside. "Did you bring the Paparazzi, Paul?"

"No, managed to get here unnoticed I think."

"Please ... come in."

The tiny flat smelled of oil paint. They sat in the kitchen

and drank coffee. Bruno pulled nervously on a cigarette. "So, you are all better now?"

"Almost. I have a few pins holding my legs together."

"Yes, I read about that. And you, *we*, are famous. You got the whole world looking for themselves. It's the new craze. The biggest craze since the Church of the Black Butterfly was formed. You have started another religion perhaps?"

They laughed together as if they were old friends and then the German became serious. "It is a pity about the others."

"Yes … and I could be Wendell, you know."

Bruno shook his head. "It's unlikely."

"But possible."

"Yes, anything is possible. Look at us."

The visitor was quiet for a moment. His mind seemed to be on something else.

Bruno cleared his throat. "You did well to survive."

"Well, I was lucky and Wendell forgot his own theory."

Bruno stubbed his cigarette and pulled another out of a pack on the table. "That we are all the same?"

"Yes, if he had a history of violence then so would I, and you, too, of course."

Bruno nodded and began to speak.

"Wait, I have something to say, if I can remember."

The German sucked on his cigarette and waited patiently.

After some contemplation, Paul spoke. "*Wendell hat es unrecht. Wir sind nicht Kopien. Wir sind Brüder.*"

Bruno clapped his hands in delight. "Yes, Wendell was wrong. We are not copies, we are brothers."

Paul reached into his jacket pocket. Something flashed in his hand as he got up. "I never did get on with my brother, did you?"

Bruno jumped up and pushed the table into Paul as he stepped back from him. "You were right, Viggo," he called quickly.

Paul swivelled in shock, waving the knife unsteadily. In the hallway behind him, a group of people were forming. As they filed out of the living room he realised that they must have been there all along: waiting silently … listening. The small kitchen filled up quickly. Paul backed away until he came up against the window frame. They stopped a yard away from him. Those that couldn't get into the room stretched their necks to see over the others. They were young and thin, old and fat, but they had a terrible similarity and their silence was unnerving. Bruno squeezed around the table and put his arm on a young man's shoulder.

"Viggo said you would do this and I disagreed."

"Is this everyone on the list?" Paul croaked, trying to buy time.

"No, not all. Some were like you and we are still looking for the others. The world has changed forever, Paul; the age of the *multividual* is here. We must adapt to survive. Imagine what a person might achieve if they could be in a hundred different places at the same time."

"It won't work. You're still a group of individuals whatever you say."

"No, when we are finished searching, we will decide on a composite name and become a true *multividual*. The only individual here is you."

Paul looked for forgiveness in the familiar faces surrounding him, but he knew better. "Fuck you all," he said wearily and pointed the knife.

They fell on him.

# FOREVER IN FOCUS

Lyman Dollie washed the blood from his hands in an extravagant froth of soapy water. He always used too much soap because, despite spending a fortune on trying to get some decent water plumbed into the hacienda, it was still dirty and he didn't like to be reminded of failure, however small that failure was.

He was troubled by the call he had just received. Whoever this Hawthorne character was – it would come to him – he knew the secret of the Texan's obsession and in the worst of scenarios, may have blabbed it to just about anyone. As Dollie made his way back upstairs, he rang Garcia, caught in the swing of two very different feelings: buoyant that the process some of his people had been developing was such a resounding success, yet livid that there might be a network of individuals, however pathetic they may be, plotting against him.

"Get the four by fours out; we're heading to Iquitos in thirty." Dollie walked briskly through his open-plan house and sat at a wicker table in front of the huge one-way window that looked over the front of his property at Santa Clara. It was exactly midday. One of his housemaids came through with his lunch: raw strips of prime Argentinean beef marinated in soy sauce, ginger and chillies, and a bowl of wilted pak choi. He forked cabbage into his mouth as he ruminated. Hawthorne was an Englishman, he seemed to remember. Dollie had hundreds of people in his employ, just in Peru alone, but he always remembered anyone he had met. He had learned a technique to do so during hypnotherapy. Yes, it was coming back to him now; he was a tutor, a drunkard and a pederast. How did he know the truth about the black butterfly? It was a revelation that was puzzling, disturbing even. But he didn't need to worry. They had the son of a bitch's photograph, so Dollie would get everything out of the Englishman; that was one thing he could be absolutely sure of.

He dropped a succulent piece of steak into his mouth and sat back. The agreeable hum of the air conditioning comforted him and he closed his eyes for ten minutes.

They came into Iquitos in a tumble of dust just under an hour later. Garcia drove and Isaacs, who had been assisting Dollie in his basement when they got the call earlier, was sitting beside his boss like a loyal guard dog.

"You send that ole boy back home before we left?" Dollie asked him, lowering his sunglasses.

"Yes I did, boss."

"How was he feeling about it all when he lit off?"

Isaacs rubbed his chin in contemplation, looking for the right words. "I'd say contrite and grateful would describe his outlook."

Dollie didn't have to join in on torture sessions as he had done that morning, but he made a conscious effort to do so from time to time. He didn't really care for the violence, but it showed those working for him that he was not to be fucked with. This time it had been a local businessman who had been a bit too vocal about his ill feeling toward Dollie and Emerald Earth.

"Well, I'm sure his remaining eye will see a lot clearer now." Dollie remarked.

The car pulled up outside a peeling colonial building to the north of town. Dollie jumped out and studied the duck-egg-blue walls and ornate, pink fretwork. He breathed the warm moist air in steadily as Garcia and Isaacs checked the doorways.

Inside, they passed two guards and went through a dark corridor which smelled sour and stuffy.

The Focus Room was behind a heavy steel door opened by a keypad, but was much less dramatic-looking than its name suggested. The ground floor of the building had been knocked out for the most part and rebuilt. The long, narrow room was lit with stark sodium lighting at the front. Two banks of Mackintosh computers ran along desks against the walls. Half of them were manned by young men. About halfway down, the light softened and then faded out completely. A young Peruvian man in jeans and a Houston Oilers T-shirt came out of the gloom to meet the three men. He looked tired.

"Is he ready, Raphael?" asked Dollie abruptly.

"Yes." The man skipped to stay up with Dollie as he marched past. "After the mandatory six hours he started to question me about the black–"

"What did he ask?"

"What did I know about it, that sort of thing."

Dollie stopped behind the large digital projector, lit from above by tiny spotlights. He rolled his hand in front of him. "And?"

"After three more hours, he broke. I couldn't believe what I was hearing but ... you know best."

"Damn straight I do." Dollie looked up at the film being projected onto the back wall. The image was of a poorly lit, ramshackle room. There were cabinets bursting with books against the walls. A wooden table sat in the centre of the room with an easel on it. Unfinished paintings littered the floor. A man was sitting on the floor beside the table, running his fingers through the wet paint on a canvass. He spoke without looking up. "Here comes Dollie ... Dollie, Dollie, Dollie."

"How do you know about the black butterfly, Hawthorne?" asked Dollie.

Hawthorne looked up, but not at the men; he couldn't see them. "I told that little shit! Now get me out of here!" he demanded.

"I want to hear it from you and then you can go. I swear on that."

Hawthorne got to his feet unsteadily, sucked some paint from his fingers and then spat it on the floor in disgust. "I don't understand why I can't get out of my own flat." His voice rose and fell in a weary despair. "The doors don't open, the windows won't break …"

"Tell me or you'll never get out," Dollie said flatly.

Hawthorne began to wander his room aimlessly, kicking at objects as he spoke. "I overheard something you said once, that's all."

"When?"

"A few weeks ago."

"Where?"

"There was a party at your house. I don't know what it was for."

Dollie sighed. "First off, you wouldn't get no invite to any occasion of mine. Second, I don't talk about my business at no God damn parties … not ever!"

"But you did. This fellow walked away from the guests with you, right out to the fence of your property. I was there in the trees. I'd been there–"

"Bullshit!"

"–all day."

"What the hell for?"

"Because I'm nosey. I knew you were having a party and I couldn't help myself. You were whispering, but I've got this voice amplifier, handy for snooping. I couldn't believe it at first, but the more I researched the myth afterwards …" Hawthorne sighed. "I just wanted a bit of info I could make some money on."

Dollie looked away and his fists clenched and unclenched rhythmically. He turned back to the man projected onto the wall. "Who did you tell?"

Hawthorne sat down. "Nobody, I swear."

"You must have ... a secret like that; it's too big to hold on to for long. Who did you tell?"

"You swore you'd let me go if I told you how I knew."

"I lied, shit for brains!" Dollie's words were thick and poisonous, like spilt axle grease. "You will never leave that room."

The Englishman looked up, his eyes spinning in terror. "I'll break out," he said doubtfully.

"You already tried that, remember?"

Hawthorne laughed and threw his glance across the room at one of the oil lamps. "I'll burn this place. You'll get nothing more from me ... do you hear me?" His voice rose to a cracked scream.

There was no movement from Dollie, just his words, implacable, relentless, and logical. "Last year, I had photographs taken of all my employees. Do you remember that? That camera's quite something. It doesn't record an image of you; it takes a part of you."

The air in the room was electric now. The young projectionist, even Garcia and Isaacs, they were all shifting a little uneasily. Dollie was doing what nobody had ever been cruel enough to do before: explaining the fine detail of a predicament too terrible to contemplate, to the victim himself.

"That part of you is then fed into this clever machine and here you are. The real Hawthorne is over yonder, on the other side of town. He might be feeling a mite sickly tonight cuz of what's happening here, but he won't know why. He's lucky; he can and will die soon enough. You cannot; you're just a slice of his soul that we can question forever." Dollie turned from the man's sobbing. He addressed the projectionist. "I'll be back in the a.m. and I want names."

They came back next morning at seven. The projectionist Raphael was slumped in a recliner by the entrance to the Focus Room. He was nursing a coffee. He stood up and rubbed his stubble when Dollie walked in.

"Lucito Morales, Howard Arizapana, Capac Huevo, Eduardo Castaneda and Moises Quispé," he said wearily, reading from a crumpled piece of paper.

"Who?"

"They are butterfly boys. Hawthorne's got a – *had* a – thing for boys."

"Anybody else?"

"Nobody."

"You're sure."

"Positive. Here are the recordings of the night's interview." He handed over a disc, which Dollie gave to Isaacs. "Check it out."

"Shall we go fetch these kids?" Isaacs asked.

"No … they're no threat, but we might put a watch on them and see where it takes us."

As they left the building, Dollie saw a figure across the road holding something in the air above his head. The sunlight flashed in his eyes and he lifted his hand quickly.

"Who was that?" The figure, a boy, he thought, had disappeared.

Isaacs looked across the road. "I didn't see–"

"Go, you idiots!"

By the time they came back, it was raining. Dollie watched them shrugging through it as they crossed the road. "You lost him."

"Didn't even see him," said Garcia, and Dollie slapped him across the face hard.

"If brains were leather, you wouldn't have enough to saddle a flea."

"What do you want us to do?" Garcia asked sheepishly.

Dollie blew a sigh. "Nothing I guess."

Isaacs opened the passenger door of the four by four and waited.

"That's weird; it's raining quite hard but the sun's still out," commented Isaacs. Dollie looked to the blue vault above him. "I guess the devil's beating his wife again."

That afternoon, Raphael awoke from a fitful sleep. He checked his watch and bleary-eyed, stumbled from his sweaty flat just off the Plaza de Armas and made his way to the east of the city. He stopped at a small roadside cafe on the way and ordered *caldo de gallina*. As he spooned the soup, his eyes, hidden behind mirrored sunglasses, carefully scanned the busy street. Revitalised by his late breakfast, he moved on again. He took a long, circuitous route and moved in fits and starts, sometimes loitering at shops, at other times ducking down alleys and waiting in the shadows thrown beneath rusting balconies.

The two men were waiting in a disused railway station in the Pevas district. Dogs scattered as Raphael came onto the platform, skipping away through muddy puddles and disappearing into the building's carcass through broken doorways. The boy with the holdall was another young Mestizo, a close friend of Raphael's. He got to his feet and they shook hands.

"Did you catch him, Daniel?"

The boy smiled broadly. "I did."

"Him alone and not the bodyguards?"

"Yes."

"You've checked?"

"Of course."

Raphael clapped him on the back. "Well done! Thank you!

Well done!" He began to laugh and the other boy joined in, relief and excitement overtaking them for a moment. "I can't wait to ruin that gringo bastard."

The old man, who had been sitting quietly, suddenly spoke in Yagua.

"What did he say?" asked Raphael.

"He is asking when you can interrogate Dollie."

Raphael shrugged. "It will have to be soon. They take pictures of all of us, once every three months, for interrogation, to check our loyalty."

Daniel whistled quietly. "A little piece of your soul every time? You paid a high price for this brother."

Raphael's eyes filled up for a moment and then he composed himself. "It's true I have, but it was the only way."

"When is the next check?"

"Mine will be in six weeks. I will question him before then and disappear," he tried a smile again but it wouldn't surface.

The Yagua chief stood up. His grass skirt rustled as he came over. He spoke again at length.

"He says he needs to know Dollie's routine and Dollie's knowledge of the black butterfly. Also, any codes or passwords for his house at Santa Clara ... anything you can get."

Raphael looked at the old man seriously. "Tell him I will meet him here in one month at the same time and he must take me with him into the jungle. It's the only place I might be safe."

Daniel handed over the holdall with the camera in it.

"How did you get this thing out of there anyway?"

"It's a big, old building. The brickwork is rotten at the rear and I broke a hole in it, just enough to squeeze the camera through. Their arrogance is a weakness; all that security out front but nothing at the back."

Daniel smiled in undisguised admiration. "What would you have done if they had needed the camera yesterday?"

"I would have run ... and been caught." Raphael swallowed hard and left without another word.

★ ★ ★

... "Stop right there, Quispé! Do you hear me?"

Moises felt his shoulder being shaken and lifted his head. He turned in his chair, suddenly aware of how his eyes burned, how dry his mouth was from all the talking and the pulse of deep pain from the ruin of his left hand.

Lyman Dollie was already up and standing by the door, whispering urgently to Garcia and Isaacs. The two men took their orders and left the hut quickly. Wendell got up and spoke to Dollie quietly for a few moments. The Texan shook his head as though he didn't want to hear the other man's words.

"This here changes everything," he muttered angrily as he turned back to Moises. He jabbed his finger at the butterfly. "How can that be on there, boy? How?"

"I don't know. Did it happen this way?" Moises asked. His head was banging.

"As far as I can recollect, and just thinking about what it could mean makes me as nervous as a whore in a church." The Texan placed the voice recorder on the table and sat beside the boy. "It confirms that all the stories are true, I mean, don't it?"

"Maybe."

Dollie kicked Moises's leg. "You better not be holding out on me or I'll drive you to hell myself and pay for extras."

Moises became aware of some activity outside his hut. He could hear orders being given in measured voices. Beams of harsh, white light passed over the hut, slicing the small building into cool strips as they came through the wooden slats. Garcia and Isaacs came back and started to move the microscope carefully from the table. Moises instinctively moved to stop them and Garcia grabbed his right hand and slapped the stump of his little finger against the table top. A searing flash shot through his fingers and up into his lower arm, pulsing like an electric eel trapped between the bones. He bent over and the world grew vast and shrank away as he blew through the spikes of pain. Dollie handed Moises a cloth and watched him wipe his face. The butterfly was taken from the hut.

"Where are we going?" Moises asked.

"Back to my hacienda; you'll read through the rest of the stories there."

"I won't do it."

Dollie got up and Moises flinched. The big man stood in front of him staring at the hut floor, a lugubrious look on his face. "You will," he said absently. "Besides, don't you want to see Hawthorne again?"

Moises doubted his ears. "Not in this way."

"It's the only way you got since I killed him."

"*Mama selva, dame fuerza!*"

"Quit saying that, it's aggravating. First off it was Hawthorne, then you, and now this Raphael. He did go missing as well … Jesus!"

Dollie moved to the door, opened it and turned to glare at Moises. Moises got up slowly and walked outside. Wendell followed him. Two large motorboats sat purring at the water's edge. Powerful arc lights swung across the water in front of them, tearing strips out of the night. Wherever they lingered, insects boiled in the white beams. The Texan stopped Moises a few feet from the house. "Sit here a piece, we ain't quite ready."

Moises crossed his legs on the cold, hard mud of the street and cradled his damaged arm with his good one. A faint breeze rippled his shirt and brought goose bumps up on his bare legs. He ignored the activity around him and focussed on the full moon, hanging above them all like a huge, silver eye staring out of the void. Thousands of tiny stars, cold and sharp, twinkled around it. *Mama Quilla* had always held a strong fascination for him. His father had once told him that she cried tears of silver when sad. These fell to earth and hardened for men to find and treasure. Moises longed to be sitting up there on her serene surface, free from men and the things they demanded of him. And yet now, even she wasn't free of man's destructive nature was she? He thought of Gabriella and shivered.

The German, Wendell, came over and sat on the floor next to him. "What makes you pick the stories you read?" he asked, staring off into the darkness.

"I don't know. I feel a pull and then they appear."

"Have you ever been to London?"

Moises gave a tired laugh. He felt a strange mixture of pity and disgust for the man sitting next to him. He was feeling new emotions all the time, he realised, and new insights. He gestured towards the sky with his head.

"No, I have not been to the moon either. Hawthorne told me about his trips to London and I watch the movies."

"Do you have control over the stories?"

"Of course not."

Wendell stood up. "Come, we are leaving now."

Dollie ushered Moises into the prow of the second boat a few minutes later and left him with Garcia and Isaacs. Moises sat there shivering, the ceaseless throbbing of his hand and the dense smell of the river making him feel nauseous. He wondered what time it was. In three hours from now they would be in Iquitos, at Dollie's hacienda. Moises thought about Hawthorne and wet himself, the water warming his thighs briefly.

The deck vibrated as the boat's engines were throttled up and they pulled out and headed up river. After an hour, Dollie brought Moises some black coffee and a small plate of peacock fish. He sat beside Moises sipping meditatively, as the boy bolted down the raw fillets and tipped the lemon juice into his parched mouth. The earthy taste of the fish brought back memories of those rare, special days when his father would allow Moises to come fishing with him and Moises's older brother, Mayta. He put the plate down and clasped the cup in both hands, taking quick gulps, wincing at the heat. Afterwards, he felt a little better, although his hand pulsed intermittently with a wild pain, despite a second injection given by Isaacs when they boarded the boat.

A table was set up on deck with a light over it. Dollie went away for a few moments and the speed of the boat slowed. He came back with Wendell, who was carrying the butterfly and the microscope. Wendell placed it on the table.

Dollie waved Moises over. "Come on, back to the grind. You can read for another hour and then I might let you rest till morning."

Moises shuffled over miserably and stood beside Dollie. The Texan looked up from where he sat at the table, a quizzical, half-smile on his heavy face.

"What's on your mind?"

"What happened to the other boys?"

"I put a spy on every one of them a while back. When we heard you had the butterfly …" Dollie pointed out into the darkness flying past the boat. "Well, the jungle has them now. It accepts all gifts doesn't it, Moises?"

Moises nodded. He remembered how, when Hawthorne was drunk or stoned, he would promise to take Moises to England for a holiday. In those moments, the two of them would discuss going to the pub, walking around the park in a town called Luton, how they intended to eat ice cream and visit the museum there, and feed bread to those strange birds called swans.

Now Moises realised that Hawthorne had made the same

promises to Lucito, Howard, Capac and Eduardo. He pictured their faces when Dollie's men ended their bleak lives: filled with surprise, terror, gratitude even. Why hadn't he realised it before? All the children here, him included, were trapped forever, like pigs in cages waiting to be milked. Only the men who owned them could set them free, with the swish of a knife or something worse.

Moises put his hand on the back of the chair to steady himself. The hatred in him was a beautiful thing: huge and clean and dark, like an endless shaft cutting through his mind, into which he could empty all of humanity.

"My brother, Mayta, he liked Peacock fish, too."

"Hell, good for him." Dollie said. "Me? I got a soft spot for rainbow trout, but they ain't available down here. What's your point?"

"He's dead ... *muerto*."

"You will be, too, if you don't park your stupid ass."

Moises sat down and gladly put his eyes to work ...

# THE JENNY MUSEUM

It took fifteen years for Richard to pluck up the courage to return to Luton. It seemed appropriate to go down on Jenny's birthday, which fell on the last Friday in March, so he booked the Thursday and Friday as holidays and spent the month prior worrying about whether he should be making the trip at all.

The week before he left became extremely busy. Richard hadn't planned it that way; he wanted to be relaxed for the trip, but something came up that he couldn't put off until afterwards. He rarely slept well and the heavy workload coupled with nervousness at returning to his hometown meant that his sleep was disturbed even further. By Thursday morning, he was shattered.

Richard rose at six and found his car slick with icy dew. He packed it and stood with his hands on the open boot lid for a couple of minutes, staring at the two suitcases, watching his breath billow over them like primeval fog. His thoughts were doughy and unfocused; he hadn't slept well at all: the witch dream again. He slammed the boot shut, went back into the house, took a couple of sleeping pills and slept through until late afternoon.

The route from Norwich was knotted in road works, exactly as it had been all those years ago, and Richard drove it thoughtlessly, as if it were a journey he made every day. At a service station on the outskirts of Thetford, he filled a 5-gallon can with petrol and put it back in the boot.

He approached Luton along the A505 and felt his heart

flare like a strip of heated magnesium suddenly exposed to oxygen as he passed the Vale Crematorium. It was the biggest cemetery in the town. His mother had been burnt there. Richard had paid to have her ashes saved, thinking he might spread them at some place she held a particular fondness for, like they did in all those TV dramas. But he had never bothered to pick them up.

He wondered if Jenny's parents had a plot for her on the site. Could you do that when there wasn't a body to bury or burn? He resisted a strong urge to turn in and look for it.

There was no need to drive through the town centre, but he was curious. A Cineplex stood where the old Co-op used to be, some pubs had died or changed names, all the petrol garages seemed to be car washes now: innocuous changes, which couldn't stop a sickly nostalgia welling up in his throat.

The guest house he had booked was just across the road from Wardown Park and the museum. The landlady, Mrs Macdonald, led him up the steep, narrow stairs to his room.

"Where do you hail from then, Mr Jet?"

"Luton, but I've been away for some years."

"I thought as much; that accent hasnae changed, has it?"

"No, I guess not."

The stairs turned sharply near the top and Richard got stuck, the meat in a suitcase sandwich. Mrs Macdonald watched from the top of the stairs, a tight smile on her lips.

"Are you alright there?"

"Yes ... fine." Richard lurched forward as he freed himself from the bottleneck, sending a rain of magnolia woodchips onto the carpet. He squeezed past her into the unremarkable little room and hoisted his cases up onto the bed. The woman looked from him to the suitcases.

"What do you do for a living, Mr Jet?"

"I'm a chemistry teacher."

"A professional man. I expect you're visiting friends or family?"

"Yes, something like that."

They regarded each other for a moment. Richard pushed at the bridge of his glasses.

"Well," she said finally, "dinner's from six till seven p.m., but I need to know if you'll be wanting some."

"I'll just have breakfast here if that's okay?"

She nodded. "Breakfast from seven thirty till nine. No later."

Like many tall people, Mrs Macdonald unconsciously hunched her shoulders. Her hair was thin and over-lacquered, and as she leaned forward, rattling off her spiel, sunlight from the landing window behind her turned it to smoke. To Richard, she looked like an ancient, desiccated witch. But, then, he saw witches everywhere.

"Will you be needing anything else?"

"No thanks. That's fine."

"Right you are then." She let the weighted door swing shut behind her.

Richard blew a long sigh through his teeth and unpacked his Antler Weekender case while he waited for the kettle to boil. He didn't open the older suitcase. Drawing the curtains against the harsh glow of the street lamps, he sat and sipped a weak tea. Around him, magnolia walls, chintz furnishings and fussy mediocrity: a trait he had come to expect in such establishments.

The bed was low and lumpy. Richard took a couple of sleeping pills and lay on his back, arms crossed over his chest, like a man waiting for tear-streaked faces to shuffle past. A large, delicate spider was moving across the emptiness of the ceiling with slow precision. *What a fate*, he thought, *to pace one's life out across such an unremarkable landscape.* Soon, tears were pulsing steadily down his cheeks and a dismal weariness overtook him. He mumbled Jenny's name long into the night.

Richard woke before five the next morning and sat by the window, watching the world shiver away the spell of darkness. Eventually, he heard movement downstairs and forced himself to have a tepid shower. He wore a black suit and tie, items bought specifically for the occasion, and spent ten minutes getting his Windsor knot just right.

The dining room was empty. It smelt of sour fat. Drab prints of hunting parties crowded the walls, like windows into a world where people still took themselves seriously. Mrs Macdonald was very cool when taking his order, only coming to life when two young lads came down for breakfast. She then spent most of her time hovering around their table: a grotesque flirtation in which she laughed loudly and far too often. This morning, her hair was flattened at the crown like a crop circle and whenever she went to the kitchen, the boys laughed at her. She didn't notice.

Richard ate a little of the rubbery sausage, shattered the bacon and slid the jellyfish egg around for a few minutes – noticing there were dried remnants of the egg's ancestors in the fork tines – before returning to his room to fetch the old suitcase. It was large, constructed of stiff, black leather with metal reinforced corners and was adorned with stickers from all of the towns he had visited over the years. Two tan straps buckled over the top. The buckles and the metal handle were rust-bitten.

"How much further?" Jenny was blowing hard as she leaned into the steep, tree-studded hill.

"Here … just behind these bushes." Richard reached a bramble bush in an area of sunlight between trees. He looked around to see if anyone was nearby and then disappeared. Jenny found him sitting beside a hole he must have dug on a previous visit. His legs were splayed around a big, open suitcase. In it there was a blue hand towel, a cloudy, amber soap bar – the type Richard's mum preferred – a tin of creamed rice and one of plum tomatoes, a box of matches and some shampoo sachets. Richard picked one up.

"I took these from the guest house we stayed at in Southend." He pushed at the bridge of his glasses. "What do you reckon? It's not a bad start, is it?"

Jenny smiled nervously. "Are we really going to run away?"

"Yes, but we need more stuff. What can you get?"


It was a bright, cool day. The sky was scattered with perfectly plump cumuli, like a giant Magritte reproduction, but the old Victorian building held its damp shadows stubbornly close. The museum was just opening when Richard passed under its portico at precisely nine o'clock. The man who opened up gave him a quizzical look as he passed through the tall, glass doors. Richard guessed they didn't get much custom first thing on a Tuesday morning and he did strike an improbable figure with his starchy funeral suit and battered old suitcase.

Richard looked around the museum interior in excitement, picking up memories. He passed through the archaeology section first, his cold footsteps echoing around the glass display cabinets painfully. Some of the rooms had been extended, but the overall themes appeared very similar to what he remembered. Richard recognised the cut away of a Saxon dwelling: arrowheads of flint and rusting iron neatly arranged in velvet cases like ancient cutlery sets. There were plastic dinosaur dioramas and the ubiquitous ammonites. Two interactive touchscreen displays had been added, almost, it seemed, as a within-budget concession to the modern world.

There was a room celebrating the history of hat making in

the town, decorated in the blue and orange of the local football team. Beyond that, in the Military Room, there stood the same life-size model of a Chindit soldier burning a leach from his arm with a cigarette. Jenny had hated leaches and Richard teased her about it every time they came, which was quite often during the summertime. It was a crazy thought, but he felt he could see something like recognition when he looked into the soldier's eyes.

He moved to the next room, which always housed exhibitions by up and coming local painters. After studying them in a kind of stupor for a while, he came back to himself, knowing he had to get it over with. Slowly, he climbed the broad, oak staircase to the first floor and put the suitcase down. He realised it was the first time he had ever been up there alone. The corridor was about 30 feet long. At the far end was a dark, glass-fronted room. His heels tapped holes in the thick silence as he made his way towards it.


Jenny squeezed Richard's hand so tightly he nearly cried out as he listened to his own quick breaths and the squeak of her plimsolls on the polished, wooden floor. Behind the glass ahead of them was a waxwork of an old Victorian woman sitting alone in her living room, busy with some needlework. Reflections slid and fractured off the glass as they edged nearer. The woman's pale, smooth face appeared to lift in a shuddery movement; Richard saw the shake of a withered arm, a sharp needle catching light … He let out an odd noise and Jenny screamed. They turned in panic, pushing and pulling at each other as they bounded down the curved, wooden staircase, past the stunned curator and out into the breathless sunshine. They bent over, hands on hips, fear making them giggle in the centre of the immaculate lawn.

"What did you see?" asked Jenny.

"Shit!" Richard muttered, staring into the empty room. He

peeled his hands from the cool glass and watched the prints fade away like disheartened ghosts.

The curator was silver-haired and wore a crisp, white lab coat. Richard found him sorting through postcards in the tiny gift shop.

"The old lady?" the man asked. "Or the witch!" His hands curled into claws and he moved forward, flashing a wall of teeth that would never need flossing. Richard recoiled in horror.

"You're worse than the kids, you are." The man laughed, but a look of concern was growing on his ruddy face. "I was only joking, mate."

"Yes I know," Richard said unconvincingly. "We used to call her that back in the old days."

The old man began stacking sweet-sized rubbers with pictures of the museum stamped on them. "Ah well, she always had quite an effect on the children." He straightened up. "Gone for refurbishment, actually. She's getting a bit shabby after all these years."

Richard left and the curator's voice stopped him at the door. "I'll tell her you called. You never know, she might come and give you a visit." The man's laughter followed him out into the park.

He sat on a bench by the boating lake, a little shaken by his experience in the museum. Was it a coincidence that the witch wasn't there on the very day he had returned?

*It's just a waxwork. She's not a witch. She doesn't know you.* Richard ran the words around his head like a mantra for a few minutes until he almost believed them. He then rang Mrs Pity. When he had first decided to contact Jenny's mother he imagined she might be difficult to trace, but he found her at the first attempt, in the same house she had received the terrible news twenty years before.

"Are you sure it's going to be okay?"

"Yes, fine."

"I mean, if it's too–"

"No, no, it will be nice to see you." There was a strained quality to the woman's voice; politeness, the habit of a lifetime, still overriding her true feelings.

"I'll be there in half an hour … if you're sure?"

"Yes, I'm very sure, Richard. See you soon."

Richard put his mobile away and sat for a few moments, watching the swans drift on the water. He was excited about meeting Jenny's mum after all this time and wasn't sure if that was the wrong feeling to have. Jenny was always with him, of course, but he only had one photograph of her and he couldn't seem to feel her anymore, or remember her voice. He looked for her in the faces of strangers. He hoped that somehow he could re-establish a connection with Jenny through her mother; that something would leak from Mrs Pity when he looked into her eyes or listened to her voice.

The house was the third in a long terrace. You could always tell the ones that had been bought from the council: they were double-glazed. Mrs Pity opened the door as he approached it, looking like an effigy of the real Mrs Pity, the one he remembered. Age had shrunken her. She wore black leggings, the type that hook over the heels, and he couldn't see any evidence of her legs touching the stretched nylon. Her pale, round face popped out of the cream fleece, smiling, and there was a fierce concentration on her features, as if it were taking all her strength to hold the muscles in position.

"My goodness, you've got so tall." Mrs Pity grabbed his sleeve to test the quality of the material.

"Very smart."

Richard shrugged, pushing at the bridge of his glasses. "I just thought it was suitable today."

"Yes, it's very thoughtful, thank you. How are you anyway?"

"Fine, and you?"

"Fine." She opened her arms and they hugged awkwardly.

He put the case down in the hall and looked around: more fake mahogany and magnolia walls. Mrs Pity showed him into the fussy living room and offered him tea. The room smelt of lavender furniture polish and years of cigarettes. She left him and he took a closer look at all the photographs of Jenny. There were none of Jenny standing proudly beside her first car, none of her posing, knife in hand, over her twenty-first birthday cake, no nebulous shots of her wedding day, or one of her looking pale and bleary eyed, holding her first child to her chest. In the majority of them, she wore a school uniform. She had a wide, tentative smile and lank hair cut into a lopsided bob. Richard remembered her father used to cut it to save money.

Above the fire was a large oil portrait of Jenny in an ornate gold frame, something her parents had obviously commissioned after her disappearance, a concentration of all the photographs in the room, rendered by someone of limited talent. It reminded Richard of the type of portrait you might see in a haunted house ride at a theme park.

"There you go." Mrs Pity set down the tray of flowery china and gestured around the room. "I couldn't have them up for years you know. Harry couldn't bear it, God rest him."

Richard nodded sympathetically.

"But I love to look at her, I really do ..."

She lit a cigarette and poured the tea through an old-fashioned strainer. Richard sipped and nodded occasionally as she reminisced. She paused only to suck at her fag and roll blue clouds at the ceiling.

"You never did get to move, then?" he asked pointlessly.

"Oh no, we couldn't leave ... not until we found her. What if she came back and we weren't here, you see? It's unbelievable really. Little Jen's still out there somewhere." She gestured furiously with her cigarette hand, whipping a ribbon of smoke across the room like a rhythmic gymnast. Her eyes began to fill up. "I'm sorry; it's the birthday and everything."

"It's fine." Richard handed her a tissue.

"It's all so unfair, though, when we were just about to emigrate."

"Yes, I know," he sighed. "Jenny was excited about moving. She talked about it a lot. I didn't want her to leave of course." He shrugged sheepishly.

"Well, you suffered as much as anyone. You were just a child for heaven's sake."

"I wish I'd stayed with her when she went back to the museum that day."

The old lady shuffled uncomfortably, eyeing him through the smoke like a poker player on a long losing streak. "Nobody noticed her go back into the museum alone, that's what I don't understand."

Richard held her gaze, despite his discomfort. "I wish I could tell you what happened. I've gone over it so many times in my head. Jenny wanted to go back one more time. I didn't want to…"

He couldn't blame her. The police had grilled him quite hard after Jenny's disappearance because he had been the last person to see her. The only witnesses who came forward at the time said they had seen Richard and Jenny in the museum and playing in the park. There was nothing else to go on, no clothing or physical evidence of any kind. Even if there had been, it was 1981, before the advent of DNA profiling and the like.

The clock on the wall broke the awkward silence. Mrs Pity waited for the twelve chimes to finish. "Right," she said, pushing herself up from the table. "That's my cue. Do you fancy a real drink?"

Richard was slightly appalled. "Erm … okay, what are you having?"

She poured a cheap whisky for him and a gin and tonic for herself. She flung the drink back and poured herself another before sitting down. He let her waffle a bit more after that. She kept repeating herself, jumping up regularly to refill her glass. Richard tried to appear interested, sipping the whisky slowly, feeling it smoulder in his empty belly. A witch's familiar slinked into the room and began weaving figures of eight between the old woman's legs. She shooed the cat away with a gentle flick of her foot.

"That's Pluto; he's the best friend I have."

Mrs Pity's blue eyes glittered. "Sometimes, you know" – her voice lowered – "when I've had a few, I feel like I can climb into the photographs. Is that crazy?"

"No … it's just wishful thinking, I guess."

She stood up and closed her eyes, fists clenched at her sides. "I'm in there with her, I hold her and tell her I'm sorry and …"

"It's okay," he said stupidly and stood up. His legs were shaking. He put his hand on her shoulder.

"… and I ask her where she is. Do you know what she says?"

Richard shook his head, willing her to stop.

"She says, 'Mummy, it's so dark … so dark …'" The old woman crumpled and he held her, his tears dripping onto her silver hair. He wondered if that was rude or not and decided it wasn't.

Afterwards, Richard poured Mrs Pity another drink and her face seemed to clear a little.

"Yes, she was excited about Australia." Mrs Pity drained her glass, crunching the ice cubes annoyingly. "If only we'd left a few weeks earlier. I wish I could just stop wishing and wishing. I'm so silly."

"Don't punish yourself," he said mechanically. His store of platitudes was running low, those remaining becoming more and more clichéd. He felt ashamed of the moment they shared, crying like that. It felt too familiar, like they had had sex or something.

"I really must be going," he finally lied. "I've a long drive ahead of me."

Mrs Pity showed him to the door and the alcohol made her move sideways and forward, sideways and forward.

"My friend will be here soon anyway. Thank you for coming."

Richard took her little ape hand and kissed it. "It has been nice."

"Packed already are you?" She gestured at the case and ran her hand over one of the frayed stickers on its side. "It's been around a bit this one," she laughed.

For a moment, Richard was struck dumb. He had wanted to show Mrs Pity the contents of the case. Otherwise, why had he bothered to bring it along? But now his nerve failed him. It would be too much for them both, he reasoned; the morning had been more emotional than he expected. He would have to visit her again and next time he would feel stronger for sure. But like a man who passes a beautiful girl every day on the way to work and swears to himself every evening that tomorrow he will ask her out, Richard knew deep down he would never have the courage.

"Yes, always organised, that's me."

Richard drove directly back to the guesthouse and lay down for a while. He felt utterly exhausted. The spider was in the corner of the room, reluctantly building a web. Its fragile movements quickly wove him into sleep.

At just after two o'clock, he woke with a cry like a child's and hoped nobody in the building heard him. He had had the witch dream again.

The dream was always the same. In it, he came home from work and she was waiting for him in the kitchen, her back to the sink, those gnarled hands braced against the worktop. Sunlight came from the window behind, throwing her face into shadow. The horror was in the details: the cups upturned in the draining rack beside her; the breadcrumbs and sugar granules scattered across the counter. He knew what would happen next but could never move quickly enough. The grimalkin was on Richard in a flash and by a terrible magic, she shrank him and spun him into the darkness of her musty cardigan. There he waited, his body wrapped in hot, itchy thread, listening to the tremulous thump of her rotten heart, knowing that one day she would take him out and do something unspeakable with him.

Richard splashed cold water onto his face for a full five minutes. He realised he would have to go home right away; all of this had been a mistake.

Mrs Macdonald was out so he concluded business with her husband: a listless creature who looked like a man who had wandered through a wilderness for years, searching for succour, and had found only his wife's mirage over and over again.

Richard stood outside the guesthouse in the small car park, kicking gravel half-heartedly, watching the museum through the swaying branches of the horse-chestnut trees that surrounded the park. When he thought of the petrol can in his boot, of how he had intended to burn the museum down with the old witch inside, he shivered. It was madness, all of it. He shouldn't be thinking this way. Maybe he needed therapy of some sort. It had been twenty years for Christ's sake.

If he could just go back, do things differently, then maybe Jenny would still be alive and he would be another person. He wanted to advise the child Richard, but he couldn't reach him. There was too much between the two of them: a chasm of darkness they could only peer across wistfully.

Jenny wrapped her arms around the peeling, steel bar and fought the centrifugal force trying to rip her away from the roundabout. Richard was opposite her, whirling like the pages of a flicker book, his foot pounding the playground floor.

"Slow down, Rich, please. I want to go back to the museum."

"Not unless you promise to run away with me."

Jenny could feel the pressure in her neck and back building as she struggled to hold her head up. Her shoulders glowed with pain. Richard's face blurred and flew from her eyes. She blinked rapidly, hearing his foot pounding and pounding …

"Okay, okay, I will! Just please slow down."

Richard leaned back and dragged his trailing leg across the grey tarmac with a rasping stutter. They sat on the grass watching the roundabout slow down, waiting for the fluids in their heads to settle.

"I'm so sorry, Jen." Richard touched her hand but she pulled away. He looked at the drying tears that were gumming up her eyelashes and felt sick. "I just can't believe you're going tomorrow night, all the way to Australia. I'll never see you again."

"You will," she said without conviction. "Listen, I'm going back to see the old lady one more time. Are you coming?"

He pulled at the grass between his legs and tossed it into the air, shaking his head. "Uh uh! No way!"

"Rich, you haven't really seen her move have you? She's not a witch, just a waxwork."

"Of course I have. She's after us … I know it."

"Well, I haven't seen anything. I think she's kind of creepy, but sweet as well."

"You'll be sorry if you go," he warned her, but she was already walking away.


It was teatime when Richard finally pulled off the A140 and escaped the rush hour traffic into Norwich. The avenue was stretched with long shadows. He got out of his car, shivering, and popped cracks from his stiff joints. The front door swung open when his key touched the lock. He stood for a moment with the key outstretched, frozen in shock. It was impossible that he could have left it open, wasn't it? He couldn't actually remember locking it, because he had been so preoccupied when he left home, but this wasn't something he had ever done before.

"Hello?" he called out three times and began to feel stupid. If there were a burglar … or something worse, they would hardly reply to him would they? He put down the cases and took out his phone. Richard didn't have his immediate neighbours' phone numbers, but he had Anne's, the Neighbourhood Watch co-ordinator who lived two doors up. They almost had a thing six months previously but he had backed out; he was rubbish at relationships.

Anne wasn't home. He left her a message: had she noticed anything odd while he had been away? It was pointless really. He couldn't stand outside until she came back could he? Richard listened to the occasional squeak of the door as it shifted in the wind, unable to force himself through it, and recalling the old curator's mocking words, he was suddenly convinced. He imagined the witch circling the cauldron-black sky, sniffing at the wind, working through the filigree of smells in the atmosphere and occasionally catching the tiniest note of him, edging closer and closer every night until …

*She's here.*

With great effort, he pushed the thought away, but his body still wouldn't move.

*What if she's actually here?*

A newspaper boy entered the garden. The crackle of his tracksuit made Richard jump. He took the free local paper from the boy's hand and the spell seemed to break.

"Stupid," he said as he closed the door behind him, but his heart was banging as he turned into the kitchen. The dripping tap mocked his empty fears. He went straight to the cellar door, unlocked it and released the large deadbolts. Uneasily, he tapped Jenny's birth date, 28371, into the alarm keypad. He kept looking over his shoulder as he descended the stairs, half expecting the witch to appear in the doorway behind him. The smell was rich and overpowering from the deodorisers, yet there was a sweeter smell underneath that caught the back of his throat, making his stomach quiver.

Richard walked the length of the quiet cellar with just the buzz of the strip lights in his ears, his hand thumping along the row of suitcases. The last one was a recently bought Atlantic trolley case in top grain red leather. He knelt down beside it and whispered, "Jenny?"

Something shifted feebly inside. Richard stared at the glossy photograph taped to the edge of the suitcase: a head shot of a ten-year-old girl, tousle-haired and bewildered.

"Why do you keep coming back?"

He looked along the line of suitcases, at all the similar photographs, and then he turned and glanced upstairs again. Maybe the witch wasn't coming; maybe she didn't know what he had done after all.

He went to the large, glass display cabinet in the centre of the room. The floor inside was scattered with withered roses. Richard pulled the photo of Jenny from the glass door and carefully stuck it back onto the old black and tan case. He opened the door and placed the suitcase inside, under the spotlights, then knelt and rubbed at one of the peeling stickers – a caravan with *Southend* written beneath it – and bowed his head.

"I'm so tired of looking for you."

# SKY OF WITCHES

That evening, the surface of 'The Talking River' broke with just a whisper. Something dragged itself up onto the rocky banks and collapsed under the huge, arched shadows of the Puente de Piedra. Above, a steady flow of cars and pedestrians passed over the old stone bridge. A faint, persistent breeze funnelled through the arches of the bridge, bringing the smell of human waste and the distant chatter of children. The shape shivered and flapped listlessly in the weak light. The creature had felt the pull of something on its innards; two of the baits excreted as it fell from the sky the previous evening had been taken. Crossing the river had taken the last scraps of energy, and it was too weak to follow the link any further. In desperation, the creature began to coo in an effort to bring the prey closer.

Two gum-chewing six-year-old boys stepped into the gloom beneath the bridge. They edged forward, pushing each other, banging their sticks to make courage. From the moist darkness, a voice, caught with phlegm, sang a strange lullaby. Too late, they saw the shape and the empty face that was making the sounds in the thickening shadows. It fell on the nearest boy as the other ran back to the box houses of the shanty town, crying about the *duende* under the bridge.

The creature swallowed what was useful, but the boy was malnourished: his dreams were dry and thin. By the time it opened its arms and let the child drop, there was just enough strength to migrate. The creature made a short loping run up the banks of the Rimac and then opened its tissue wings to let the breeze take it upwards.

The cloudless summer sky above Lima was falling into ash as the sun sank behind the mountains. The cooling air swam with translucent shapes, embryonic kites that sniffed at the fears of the population below, searching for a deep well to drink from and so a way back into existence.

In the shanty town on the slopes of San Cristóbal, behind the walls of those blue and pink and yellow houses that seemed to be fleeing up the mountain to escape their fate, the pickings were slim. But away to the south-west, the districts of San Isidro and Miraflores stank of bloated fears, and those that were able to, begged the winds to carry them there.

Javier Escobal left the Banco Continental offices as early as possible and took the Avenida San Pablo into the Victoria district of the city. He took the detour at least once a week. The guilt he always felt was never strong enough to stop him. Almost every radio station was reporting new cases of *Los Duendes Nuevos*: the frightening attacks that were occurring in the wealthier parts of the city. Although he didn't believe in *duendes*, new or otherwise, you couldn't help but be worried. People were being hurt and whatever was happening, seemed to be increasing as the summer wore on.

Javier kerbed the car when pulling up, such was the excitement that gripped him whenever he saw the black gates of *La Iglesia de la Mariposa Negra*.

He looked around nervously as he eased open the creaking gates, convinced against all logic that his mother or his sister would be waiting for him there one day. His throat dried at the thought as he walked up to the low stucco building. He paused at the entrance to admire the black steel wings, which rose from the church roof into the gritty air. What would his mother say if she did find out? It wasn't hard to guess: the good catholic man, successful bank administrator, owner of a property in one of the most desired neighbourhoods of the San Isidro district, now worshiping with the unwashed in the house of a Pagan god? Yet none of these fears stopped Javier from coming here. Because when he looked up at those wings, they seemed to beat for him, beckoning him into a world of unlimited possibilities.

The church interior was cool and the scent of orchids filled his mouth. Above the altar was a 12-foot square image, a close-up of Moises Quispé, the boy who had found the black butterfly in the rainforest near Iquitos. It was of poor quality, yet the boy's gaze was still arresting despite its choppy pixels. Javier stared into the boy's dark eyes. He wished he could see what they had seen. There were about thirty locals sitting in there, some writing on their black cards, others staring at Moises's image, pencil in hand, waiting for the magic of *La Mariposa Negra* to teach them how to write.

Javier Escobal marched to the altar and placed his hands on the cold, stone shape of the black butterfly that was cut into its surface. He closed his eyes for a few moments, letting his imagination drift, then picked up a pencil and a butterfly-shaped card from the pile and found a seat.


The sign was out in the front garden again when he got home: *Se necesita muchacha.*

"Monica, what happened with Irene?" he called as he entered the house. The creak and whine of violins being played badly almost drowned out his words. "Monica? Monica!"

His wife met him at the kitchen door, wiping her hands on a towel. "They are working you too hard at that bank, Javier." She kissed him lightly on the cheek and stepped back. "What is wrong?"

Javier sighed. "What happened? Where is Irene?"

"Oh her..." She waved her towel dismissively. "I told the girl to go home early. She makes a mess of everything."

"Why the sign again? We don't need another domestic; Irene is good ... Irene is–"

"No, we need to replace her and get another. I will get your dinner." She turned away before he could reply. Javier put his hands on the door jamb above his head and sighed deeply. "*A su madre*, Monica! Why do we have to keep doing this?"

"Papa, look what we found." Virginia and Sofia were around his legs, their big eyes pleading for attention.

"How are you today *mis pequeñas*? Your violins sounded magical." He took the two small boxes that were being offered to him and looked them over. "What is this?"

"We found them, Papa ... in the garden."

They were each about the size of a regular matchbox, with tangled cobwebs hanging from them. As Javier turned one in his hand, the lid fell open. The skin on his back tightened as he ran his finger with and against the velvet-like nap.

"And in here?"

The two girls gave each other a worried look.

"Nothing, Papa."

Javier fixed them with a serious look. "Eh?"

"*Goma de mascar*. Momma took it from us, but it was okay, it tasted fine. We think it was a present from God. You see–"

Javier held up his hand. "Slow down, Virginia, slow down."

She took a gulp and reached for the cobwebbed box. "*Por favor?*"

Javier watched her climb the stairs. When she reached the top, she put her hand through the iron balusters and dropped the box. The cobweb opened into a delicate parachute and the box spun slowly to the ground at Javier's feet.

His eldest daughter smiled down at them both. "You see ... God sent us some presents."

Monica served him his dinner, prepared the children for bed and then went out for the evening. It was her bridge night. She had been going for two months now. Apparently, it was the thing to do at the moment: another disease of affectation contracted from the States. It pained Javier that his wife was becoming so stuck up; no doubt their old friends whispered '*pitucos*' behind their backs these days.

He pushed his dinner around the plate without interest. *Lomo saltado* again; the beef aggravated his bowels but Monica seemed oblivious to his complaints. In the lounge, his mother watched soap operas with the sound turned way too high and shouted expletives at the characters. He took his beer and joined her for a few minutes.

She shifted her bulk into a more upright position and immediately turned the station over as she always did; she couldn't enjoy it with him in the room it seemed. The big ceiling fan rotated hypnotically and his mother's predictable questions about his day at work mingled with the newsreaders words until he could not pull them apart. After what he considered to be an acceptable time, he made his excuses.

"I am going to check on the girls, Mama. Are you okay?"

"Of course. God is kind; he gave me you to watch over me in my old age."

He looked at her face, trying to gauge whether she was being sarcastic or not. "Okay," he said, bending to peck her on the cheek. "Can I turn it down a little? The children ..."

She fingered the remote and the sound dropped dramatically. "I don't wish to hear about these new *duendes* anyway."

Javier glanced at the television and saw a familiar scene: a hospital ward set up to house the victims of the new phenomenon that was terrifying the city. A doctor was shining a pencil light into a man's eyes. The patient, his face blank, mouth slack, showed no sign that he was aware of the world around him. It cut to a young woman on a dark suburban street. She was telling a reporter that she had seen the thing that had attacked the man – her boyfriend – in their bedroom the previous evening. Javier turned the sound back up a little, but the woman broke down as she tried to describe the attacker to the reporter.

"She is delusional," whispered Javier's mother. "It is a disease, that is all … eh, Javier?"

"Yes, it could be a virus or something; that is what the government is saying … but why all these stories?"

"Delusional," his mother repeated.

Javier patted her hand and she flinched a little.

The girls were at the bedroom window when he came upstairs, their faces stained orange by the sunset.

"*El cielo de brujas*," he murmured, joining them.

"Why is the sky full of witches, Papa?" Sofia asked.

"It is not. This is just a name for the colours you see at this time of year. Now into bed or *los duendes* will come for you." He immediately regretted his words. What had always been a myth to tease the children with, now seemed a possibility too frightening to voice.

The girls scrambled into bed.

"They live in the walls?" Virginia asked.

"Can you hear them?" Javier asked.

His daughter's eyes flicked from side to side, as if to help her ears. After a few moments, she shook her head.

"Of course not, because we had all the *duendes* removed from this house before we moved in. They live far away in *la selva* now," he said quickly, and kissed both of them on the forehead. He moved across to the window and as he closed the wooden shutters, noticed a few matchbox-sized shapes scattered across his back garden. Javier felt a cold breeze pass through his mind. He went down and on entering the garden, was overcome by the feeling again; it was very still and humid out there, everything made vague by deepening shadows. As he was picking up the boxes, the cicada stopped purring and he froze. His head swivelled back and forth, anticipating an attack from something hidden in the foliage of the borders. But what was he scared of? Before he could put any kind of name to his fear, the cicada started up again and broke the spell. He hurried back inside.

The soaps were back on in the living room, so Javier sat in the cool of the kitchen after retrieving the boxes, feeling a little ashamed of his jumpiness. He rolled a ball of the gum around in his hand and took another sip of beer. He had binned the other six.

*These things are connected to the new epidemic*, Javier thought to himself. Instinct told him that, even if the purpose of the boxes and the gum eluded him. He tried to open his mind, as the Church of the Black Butterfly encouraged him to do. The old Javier would have turned away from this problem, but he trusted his imagination now, was no longer ashamed of it. The Catholic faith could keep its reveries and the endless catechisms that constricted the mind, chained it to a rigid and archaic doctrine. When Javier took up the pen in the black church, his mind really did open up like wings and his thoughts flew. Although he would not admit it openly, he believed in what Moises Quispé had alleged. It made sense, didn't it? All these strange occurrences, all the magic and the terror reported daily around the globe. Moises had said he had read these prophecies on the wings of the black butterfly and he was trying to warn the world. Then he disappeared.

For most people, these were the ravings of a mad person and yet, logic was receding lately. Javier believed in what was replacing it. Late at night, as his family slept, he would often re-read what he had written in the black church and his cheeks would flush at how he had betrayed his faith, his wife and his country with such uncensored thoughts. And he felt free.

To understand, you had to take chances, you had to be brave. Javier popped the gum in his mouth and began to chew slowly.

It tasted fine.

He lay in bed, waiting for his wife's return, wondering about the small boxes and the chewing gum. He felt sure there was a method behind them. And as the ceiling fan spun him into sleep with cool sweeps of air, he suddenly had an idea about the gum and the threat of something unfathomable, out there in the warm darkness. Something to do with fishing, how when a bait was taken, predator and prey were linked, drawn together until ... He tried desperately to come back to wakefulness, praying unashamedly to a god he no longer believed in, to keep his daughters safe.

Before he was fully awake, he found himself on his feet, propelled to the door of his bedroom by a noise, a muffled cry perhaps, an alarm in his ears. He stubbed his toe on the door frame and stumbled through it as his mind tried to catch up, came into his daughters' bedroom and took a huge breath, stunned by what was in front of him. Sophia and Virginia were huddled beside their beds, shivering in each other's arms. Over them stood something insubstantial, yet filled with menace: a tall, swaying figure like a jellyfish suspended in rippling water. The shape shifted a little and a long, slack face turned to appraise him. He looked into the tiny eyes: black hollows that seemed to suddenly stretch away through the walls of the house, out across the Pacific Ocean and on into the endless indifference of space.

Then it was on him: a damp blanket kissing his eyes, his

mind and filling up his mouth. He tasted smoke and brine and blood, and last of all, the exquisite bite of complete hopelessness.

The hospital always smelled of sweet urine and sharp lemony disinfectant, echoes of the unending battle between thoughtless bladders and underpaid nurses. Virginia Escobal pulled her chair closer to her father's and sliced a piece of black sponge cake. She pulled the piece of butterfly wing free and held it to her father's lips.

"Eat, Papa … It's my birthday. I'm fourteen today."

The man's lips twitched and some crumbs fell onto the floor. He bit a piece off and chewed slowly, his eyes looking across the room at the colourful wall Virginia had been allowed to paint for him two years before. She put her arm around his wasted shoulder and followed his gaze.

"*El cielo de brujas*," she sighed. "The sky of witches is beautiful, no? You see the butterflies, Papa, flying away to better worlds … safer worlds than this." She pointed at the scene she had so lovingly rendered. "Can you see the black butterfly?" His eyes moved to the right and up. "You see it …? That is your butterfly. Did you go with it, Papa?"

Virginia didn't know why she talked such stupidity; she knew that her father's essence, the best part of him, was not with the black butterfly. She had watched the creature suck it out of him and become stronger, more substantial. And then, apparently sated, the thing had fled back out of the bedroom window, like a curtain torn from its tracks and flung into the night sky by a bitter, black wind. She would not abandon her father as the others had. His visits to the Black Church caused the attack, that's what her grandmother often said. He had attracted the demon with his sacrilege. Virginia thought it was just bad luck, nothing more. The world turned on chance, but nobody wanted to believe that.

Nowadays, The Church of The Black Butterfly was the fifth most popular religion in the world and her grandmother refused to speak about it at all.

Virginia took out the newspaper, as she always did on her visits. "They have found another black butterfly, Papa, in Sumatra. That is six now." She pushed some more cake into her father's mouth, knowing that even if she baked it a thousand times, improving the recipe on each occasion, it would always taste the same to him.

# THE SHINING PATH
# TO TURTLE BAY

"It has taken two years and lots of painful negotiation, but today, Moises Quispé will finally speak at the General Assembly of the United Nations here in New York.

From day one, this has been a controversial subject to say the least and as I speak, a huge crowd of representatives from the Evangelical and mainstream Christian churches of America are gathering just four blocks from here on First Avenue to protest against what they see as a rejection of God himself. Pitted against them, on the other side of a strong police barricade, members of The Church of the Black Butterfly wave their dark flags defiantly.

Security is high here, particularly after the terrorist organisation, The Shining Path, or New Shining Path as they now like to be called, have vowed to kill Mr. Quispé before he can speak. They believe that appearing on this grandiose stage is proof that he is nothing more, and I quote, 'than a black puppet of capitalism,' reference there of course to the black butterfly that Mr. Quispé has so far refused to reveal to authorities or indeed, the general public. We have less than an hour now before Turtle Bay welcomes ..."

Moises looked away from the flat screen on the wall towards Miss Gallo, who was deep in conversation with the General Secretary and two men from the Peruvian Government. Moises didn't even know what their titles were, or care, he just wanted it all over with. His hands rolled nervously with each other on his lap like mating snakes. He stopped them and studied the nub that once was the little finger on his left hand.

It was all happening exactly as he had read it would. *So why don't I stop it? Because I am Pachamama's instrument now, her revenge upon the world.*

Miss Gallo came across the room, her leaf-green trouser suit whispering as she walked. She sat on the long, grey, leather settee beside him and took his hand. Moises's heart hammered alarmingly in his chest.

He remembered the first time she had shaken his hand, in a rundown library in Iquitos four months after Lyman Dollie had died. It had been arranged by Raphael with great difficulty; everything in this process had been long, tiring and fraught with danger. And for what? So he could be here today and watch something beautiful die …

She had taken much persuading of course. Moises had read the black butterfly for her, his eyes naturally drawn to those stories which were relevant. Within six months, she had proof of the power of the butterfly, when those things became true in the natural world. But it was his heart that Moises remembered the clearest; how it thundered when she shook his hand.

"This is your moment, Moises. I am so proud of what you have done and what you are about to do. I will help you today." It sounded like a speech she had practised, but it didn't lessen the effect one bit.

Moises turned to look into her eyes, so clear that he thought he could see his own face reflected in them. *I don't deserve to be in there*, he thought. Her heavy lips were avocado, the skin around her eyes shades of moss green.

"Today, you are Señora de la Selva," he heard himself say.

She grinned. "I am proud to be … Come on, it's nearly time."

Moises stood up, feeling awkward in his green, linen suit. He wore it so that they might take him seriously; a skirt and beads would surely have been distracting. He wanted them to listen, but he knew that he wouldn't finish the speech.

Through the long windows, he could see the East River, like a length of hammered iron under the overcast sky. He turned away from it, as he had read he would.

The corridors were high, clean and grey, pricked with numerous spotlights. Moises passed through them in a trance. The suited old men who patted his shoulder and whispered words of encouragement and the others who eyed him suspiciously; he was under no illusions as to their thoughts. The Americans, and most of the other nations, wanted the butterfly, but it was far away in the heart of *la selva*. Moises thought he might be kidnapped by the American Government at some point on this trip. Not before or during of course, because he had read about all that … but afterwards? He had attempted to avoid that possibility by arranging a helicopter to whisk him away afterwards, surrounded by Peruvian dignitaries, ecologists and as many celebrities as he could stomach. Besides, he was of no use without the butterfly and it was of no use without him; their fates were entwined now.

Raphael touched Moises's hand as he passed him and entered the vast General Assembly Hall, then Miss Gallo's footsteps went silent on the green carpet.

Moises did not look at the representatives as they turned to watch him make his way forward. He watched the woman in front of him: the swing of her arms, her hips, the slight sway of her hair, and he hated himself completely.

The tall, gold panel with the UN emblem on it loomed over him and they turned to skirt left and climb the steps to the rostrum. Miss Gallo stopped at the top and Moises heard his name announced. She stepped aside and smiled encouragingly.

Moises moved forward through the silence and placed his speech papers on the green, marble lectern. He turned to the President of the General Assembly, Secretary-General and Under-Secretary-General, who sat at the large, green table beside him. They nodded.

Moises spoke well, as he knew he would do. He told the assembly his story, with a few alterations. He told them that he believed the appearance of the black butterfly was a warning from *Pachamama* or Mother Nature, its prophecies punishments for the damage being done to the earth. And he offered the UN a deal. If swift, radical changes were made to the way man was treating the planet, he would hand over the butterfly. The words flowed from his mouth like a bleak song, sometimes booming with anger, at other times falling to a hush, such was his emotion. Yet all the time a small part of him was separated from it all, tracing the journey of the words across the paper, unable to stop the moment that was approaching steadily.

After twenty minutes of the hour-long speech, Moises stopped and took a sip of water. He looked up into the vast, domed roof above him for a second. Ringed with spotlights, its pale, marble centrepiece shone like the pupil of something unworldly. It watched him with ambivalence as he prepared to continue.

Moises cleared his throat. "The rainforests are the oldest ecosystems on this planet. They have existed for almost one hundred million years. They cover only two percent of the earth's surface, but are home to two-thirds of all living species, and almost half of all of man's medicines have come from rainforest plants.

Some people call them the lungs of the world, but they are more than this. *La selva* is the heart and the soul of this world. It represents the massive damage being done to every eco-system on earth." He paused for a second. *Why can't I stop? Why won't I?*

"Half of the four billion acres of rainforest have gone already. At present rate of destruction, there will be no rainforests by the year 2060. By then, world population is predicted to be close to ten million. It is estimated that more food will have to be produced in the next fifty years, than has been produced in the whole of human history. Who suffers? All other species on this planet, and man himself, because without diversity, where is man's soul?"

Moises felt close to tears, but they were not for himself or the planet he lived on. They were for Natalie Gallo. "I bring you the news that nobody wants to hear. Man has inadvertently declared war on the earth. We must understand that Mother Nature has already begun her response."

The words meant nothing to Moises now. They were never his anyway. He turned to Miss Gallo and called her something for the first and last time. "Natalie … I …"

Her brow furrowed and he heard a sudden commotion behind him: shouting, scuffling, and a woman's scream. *No!* He thought and turned, but Natalie stepped in front of him and over her shoulder he saw a flash of the plastic gun that had evaded the sensors, in the hands of a short, suited man running up the steps to the podium. Moises just had time to register a face, but only remembered the eyes afterwards, black and hollow like the gun barrel before it exploded. Then he heard the shots – one … two … three – the third from the security guard bringing the assassin down.

Natalie's body spun and hit him, knocking him to the ground. Her face fell into the crook of his neck, her hair over his eyes. Moises felt a hot wetness creep steadily through the fabric of his shirt and his neck slowly cooled as her breathing faded.

He began to scream.

★ ★ ★

... "Okay, Quispé, we're done for now."

The Texan lifted his arm and made a circling shape in the air above his head. He looked shaken. Moises stared at him, dumb with shock. The engines throttled up and Moises nearly fell from his chair as the boat increased speed.

When the butterfly was taken inside, Dollie gave Moises another coffee. He held it tightly. The heat seemed to soothe his damaged hand.

"What is it?" Moises asked, staring out into the darkness, his tears drying quickly in the wind.

Dollie thought for a moment. "I don't know, but I am about to go to war with it, I think."

"I will not go to New York. I–"

"Of course you won't. According to that thing I'm a dead man. No, I'm glad you read that one, so we can stop that pretty little scenario before it occurs," he blustered, but his voice sounded hollow to Moises.

Wendell sat beside Dollie, his face bright with excitement. "It's quite scary when you think about it," he said.

Dollie turned to him.

"The story just after I met him had my name and other influences from me in it. I'm sure if you looked at the other stories there would be other correlations."

"But that shit about Hawthorne happened last year and he had no knowledge–"

Wendell rose to his feet. "No, and some of it is far in the future. There is more going on here than we can understand, but some of this is the boy's doing."

Moises shook his head. "These things won't happen."

"I think they already have in some sense."

193

"Jeesus! What kinda mumbo jumbo bullshit is that?" asked Dollie.

Wendell sat back down, becoming a vague shape just outside the small pool of light from the table lantern. "I know, I know, we'll find a way around it. I just need to think. Are you going to tell him?"

"About what?" asked Dollie.

"Alice Cavendish."

"That wasn't top of my list of things to do tonight, no."

"It might help. He might have an insight somehow."

Dollie sat up, his body tense. "Go on then, you sonofabitch, tell him. I'm short on time in case you hadn't noticed."

"This creature," Wendell began, "shows up every eighty to a hundred years ... has done for as long as records have been kept. In 1926, on the outskirts of Iquitos, not far from where Señor Dollie now lives, a girl, Alice Cavendish, found a big, black butterfly in her garden. The insect was killed by a servant, but the girl's father, an English rubber baron of some note and a keen lepidopterist, kept the remains. Later, he was looking at it under a microscope with his daughter when she swore she could see writing on the wings. After some persuasion, Cavendish copied what she read down onto paper. The family were to leave the following day for Malaysia, but the girl was missing from her bed when the nanny went for her next morning. Later, they found the butterfly gone, too. Neither were ever seen again."

"The Yagua took her," Moises said.

"I believe you are right," Wendell said. "There are some uncertified reports that the girl lived with the Yagua to an old age."

"We will never understand these things."

"Did you know, Moises, that the Japanese have the myth of the white whale who sings the secrets of the world as she glides through the ocean depths? And in Indonesia, they say there's a village deep in the jungle where a giant, ancient tortoise lives. Once every thirty years, the tortoise talks for a full day without stopping. There are signs and wonders everywhere, if you care to look for them."

Moises sighed. "You cannot control the black butterfly, señor. It answers for no human."

He could not stop thinking of the things he had seen. He felt responsible. A sickening weight rolled in his stomach.

Dollie suddenly sprang to his feet and Moises couldn't help but flinch. The Texan rubbed his hands together briskly and his breath steamed in the cold night air. "We will, because we have to. I think these stories are signposts … warnings, too. I aim to make good use of them. Why did you find it, Quispé? What would be the point? To bring it to my attention, that's why. I have the power to use the knowledge in those wings." Dollie jabbed his hand in the direction of the table. His eyes glowed with fervour in the rushing darkness. He turned away and placed his hands on the prow of the boat, like a zealot in the pulpit, preaching to an empty church long after service. "It stands to reason we got to move off this planet sometime soon. It's just a matter of finding how. Something on those wings will show us, I know it. We have to keep reading."

Moises finished his coffee and watched the steam curling from the empty cup. He didn't fully understand what Dollie was talking about, but as he listened, Moises realised he should have destroyed the butterfly the moment he caught it. He glanced at Wendell sitting casually to his left, the two soldiers beyond him. They were looking out at the water, seemingly uninterested in the conversation. Watching these four men, and their utter indifference to him and his world, caused a sudden surge of rage to swell up in his chest. His mother and father, his brother Mayta, and all the others who had been killed by the actions of these people, seemed to be forgotten by everyone but himself.

"Hawthorne … he says you are director of the oil company Hevron?" Moises said, shaking with emotion.

Dollie turned and put his back to the water, his hands gripping the gunwale behind him. Dawn was coming and the sky above him was stained a filthy orange. "I do have a controlling interest in that particular company, but it ain't common knowledge. Doesn't tally with the work of Emerald Earth."

"You killed my family."

Dollie's smile was sardonic, slightly tired. "So you keep saying, but I had nothing to do with it. You people don't own this jungle. Your new president, Mr Garcia, knows that and he's a friend of mine. You better read me something I can use come morning … do you understand?"

Moises nodded and the Texan dismissed him. But as he turned to give instruction to Wendell, Moises jumped to his feet, lowered his head and ran at him. Before anyone could react, he hit Dollie full in the chest. For a moment it seemed that his charge would have no effect on the big man. Dollie grunted as if in disgust at the pitiful assault, but as he pulled his hands from the gunwale to push the boy away, he leaned back from Moises's flailing hands and the momentum of the boy tipped him to the point of no return. With a shriek, Dollie got a hand on the boy's shirt and they both went under the bow of the speeding boat. Moises was buffeted through the roiling water, and the cold sheared through his senses, stopping all thought. The terrifying weight of the boat smacked into his shoulder and he felt the propeller churn past his head with a monstrous roar, spinning him away from it violently. He surfaced coughing in its fizzing wake. As his eyes cleared, he saw the boats, already quite a way upriver, sweeping around in two graceful arcs to return for him and Dollie. Moises looked around in panic for the other man as the vicious current tugged at him incessantly. He could not see or hear any sign of the Texan. Resigned to his fate, Moises attempted to swim to the bank, filled with a certainty that if Dollie's men did not shoot him in the water, the current would take him down to the riverbed soon enough. A spotlight found him almost immediately. Bathed in blinding light, and feebly treading water, he raised his arms and waited for a bullet. It did not come. A metal hook smacked him on the shoulder and he grabbed at it gratefully as numerous voices shouted instructions. He was dragged to the hull of the boat and hoisted up, flung unceremoniously onto the deck.

Surprisingly, he was then left alone. He snorted the muddy river from his nostrils and tried to make himself comfortable, but his right shoulder protested whenever he put weight upon it. Moises sensed something was wrong with Dollie. He had heard the man crying out when the boat picked him up. There still seemed to be a lot of panic and angry shouting from members of the crew and much bustling about. The men who ran past him looked very scared.

Moises managed to crawl into the curve of the boat's hull. He drew his knees up and hugged them to him, hoping he would be forgotten forever. And remembering his most precious possession, went to the pocket in his shorts. The water-softened matchbox was still there. He took out the tasteless lump of gum and popped it into his mouth. The sky continued to lighten and with the buzz of the motors, the bark of the howler monkeys now came across the water as Moises drifted into exhausted sleep, still chewing his brother's gum.

His nose woke him: the sweet reek of human waste punctuated by the smoke of the moto-cars that were already rasping through the city streets. Moises sneaked a peek over the gunwale and saw Belen, the floating port of Iquitos, which was almost dry at this time of year. The raft homes that in two months' time would be floating 20 feet higher lay surrounded by sun-dried timber and rubbish. Above them, thatched-roofed houses leaned drunkenly in all directions on their toothpick stilts, as if gazing down on the ground in pity or longing. The doors of some had been slid open and blank-faced children sat outside with their legs dangling over the detritus. The roofs were lined with *gallinazos,* who shuffled restlessly, flapping their dusty black wings in anticipation. They were waiting, as always, for their silent partners, dysentery and cholera, to do their work on the young and the infirm.

Sometime later, Dollie approached from the rear of the boat. His face was pale and hollow. There was a sling on his left arm and the bandages were soaked a deep red. Moises saw a drop of blood fall from it to join the others streaked down the thigh of the man's trousers. The Texan stopped in front of him and grimaced. "You've got some pepper, I'll give you that much."

Moises stood up shakily. "Maybe I am not like glass."

"You'll break well enough," Dollie assured him.

The soldier behind Moises brought the butt of a carbine down on the back of his head and the boy crumpled to the deck.

## Bagua

### April 28th 1997

When The People left their tents and gathered there that morning, the boy spent an hour on his father's back, looking through the long, wooden spears that clanged against the tarmac in agitation every time an army vehicle appeared. At the head of the crowd was a loose pile of trees and shrubbery blocking the highway that his father had called *la curva del diablo*: the devil's curve. Beyond, lay 200 yards of empty road that the soldiers occasionally ventured down, calling through horns for the crowd to disperse.

The boy felt very proud up there on his father's shoulders, with the man's strong, calloused hands holding his ankles. The stiff palm leaves on the man's headdress scratched against his empty belly as the songs of the Yagua and the Wampis filled the sky. Most of The People there were young and male, dressed in cut-off jeans, T-shirts and baseball caps. But his brother and his father wore the traditional grass skirts of their tribe and had marked their faces with the scarlet juice of the achiote berry.

Just before he came down from his father's shoulders, the boy saw a long line of squat vehicles appear over the hill ahead. Beside them, double rows of soldiers marched like leaf-cutter ants down the highway. His father left him then, moving forward through the crowd, responding to calls from the front. For a while, the boy played with his older brother as the crowd murmured and swayed with a growing anticipation. This involved nothing more than the two of them pushing and pinching each other, and his brother taking him in a headlock and squeezing his nose until the boy thought it would burst. When they got bored of this, the two of them went back to shouting insults at the soldiers they could not see.

Their mother spent most of the time on her tiptoes, trying to see what was happening up ahead. But sometimes, she looked down at her youngest son, smiled and ruffled his hair. He squeezed her hand very tightly in these moments and kissed it repeatedly. Often, her face would change as she was looking at him; it would become stretched and ugly and she would go back to shouting, straining to see over the chanting crowd.

The heat had grown between the swaying jam of arms

and legs and was wringing sweat from them. The People had become a restless mass of dark, wet flesh. The boy stood in the shadows, clutching his mother's red skirt tightly. He stretched his neck back and watched the sky, trying to take his mind off the heat, his grumbling stomach and the angry shouts around him. The sun was above them now, hidden behind the great heaps of dark cloud that had been building since early morning. Occasionally, a patch would simmer and burst into a blinding lance of sunlight before darkening again. These moments always took the boy by surprise and left rings, dancing in the corners of his eyes.

The crowd surges were becoming more frequent and more violent. There was nothing the boy could do but hold onto his mother's skirt, go with it, try to stay on his feet and anticipate the response: a sudden surge back again. There was a thick, prickly atmosphere growing in the crowd and the voices were becoming more hateful. When he took a breath, the air seemed to die in his mouth. It felt like he was trapped in a dense part of *la selva* and he wanted to climb one of the trunks, clamber across the canopy and away to safety.

Out of the corner of his eye, he saw his brother manoeuvre his arm to take out a matchbox he had tucked into his skirt. The boy knew it contained a soft sweet that could be chewed many times and never disappear. A tourist had given this magic to his brother when he had visited their village.

"For me," the boy shouted, snatching at the matchbox as his brother slid it open. The older boy grabbed him by the throat and shook his head slowly.

The young boy wriggled, calling his brother the name he had heard most of the crowd shouting at the soldiers.

"*Nimbyii! Nimbyii!*"

His brother slapped him across the face once. The boy dropped his arms and hung his head. His brother smiled and took the gum from the little matchbox. He tore it in two and handed half over.

"Here!"

The boy popped it in his mouth. It was hard and tasteless.

"Thank you, Mayta," he said.

His brother's face was swallowed up as the crowd surged forward again. The boy felt a violent shove in his back and nearly fell. As the weight of the crowd swung around him, he lost his grip on his mother's skirt. Everyone was looking upwards. There were grunts and yelps of panic aimed at the sky. He caught a glimpse of what was causing the crowd's agitation: a metal truck floating in the sky to the left of the road. The truck came lower and the boy saw a man leaning from the side, cradling a large gun. There was a thump and then another; the crowd opened and something clattered onto the road. The boy watched it spin, billowing blue smoke out in every direction. His breath caught in his throat. Somebody hit him as they ran past and he fell to his knees, tears streaming from his eyes. Shapes spun and screamed in the smoke around him. The gum fell from his mouth on a string of drool and he reached for it.

Somebody lifted him up, pushed him under an arm and ran for the trees. For a second, the smoke parted and he saw the tree-line bouncing towards him through clear daylight. There was a buzz past his ear, close enough to send a shiver through him. The screams grew louder. The arm holding him suddenly loosened and he rolled in the dust at the roadside, yelping as the skin came away from his chest and elbows. He tumbled down the embankment and hit a cushion of tall grass, which bent around him like a protective fist. He did not want to get up from there. In the grass, tiny insects comforted him with their chatter. Above, there were popping noises, strange cries and the growl of motors, and he wondered if they were part of a dream he was remembering for the first time. Dark wings began beating in his mind, urging him to be as still as the dead. He watched them until he fell asleep.

Silence woke the boy. He sat up, feeling as if he had done something wrong and would be in trouble for hiding down in the grass. He brushed down his face and arms. His chest was covered in dark patches of clotted blood and dust. They burned unbearably as he got to his feet and he shook his hands and whistled at the pain. Above him there was a grey haze where the crowd had been standing. It was quiet, except for a subdued crying which fluctuated, coming in whispers and mutterings from different directions.

He saw his mother immediately. The red of her skirt took his eye at the side of the road. She was sprawled over the side of the embankment on her back, arms flung out towards him. The black hair he loved to bury his head in was spun across her face. He stared at her, feeling uneasy, willing her to move before he did. Then she did move and as her body began to shake, the hair fell from her face and he saw her mouth was ragged and enlarged, saw that somehow it had swallowed her nose. She slid backwards up onto the road and out of sight.

The boy climbed the embankment and saw a soldier pick his mother up and throw her over his shoulder. The road was a tangle of bodies, flags and broken spears. Soldiers were moving amongst the mess, nudging The People with their boots. The boy followed the man who was carrying his mother. As he reached for her, another soldier caught him from behind. The boy struggled and screamed, but the soldier put his arms around him, held him tight against the man's tough breastplate and waited for the boy to tire.

The soldier with the boy's mother over his shoulder moved down the embankment, following a line of other soldiers carrying bodies. They filed into the trees and disappeared. The boy flinched every time he heard the deep thump of something heavy being tossed into the river beyond sight. After a few minutes, the noises stopped.

Gradually, the boy stopped struggling and became quiet.

He felt dislocated from his body, as if he were hovering above it. There was a loud buzzing in his ears.

The soldier whispered that everything would be all right and stroked his head occasionally. The boy closed his eyes in exhaustion and succumbed to the arms encircling him.

Some more soldiers arrived. Their uniforms were unmarked by dust or blood, and their shields shone dully in the grainy light. The man holding the boy released his grip on him and stood up. "You must wait here," he said. "Somebody will take you soon."

The boy did not respond. He sat at the side of the road with his legs crossed, looking around, unable to focus his mind on anything he was seeing. A banner lay torn in front of him. It read, *La selva no se vende*. Beside it was the piece of gum his brother had given him earlier. He picked it up and put it in his mouth.

★ ★ ★

… Moises woke to Wendell slapping his face.

"*Mama*," he cried and bolted upright. His head throbbed sickeningly and for a second he thought he would faint. He opened his eyes and Wendell stepped back.

Mr Dollie stood over him. "Your mother isn't here. It's just me and these fellas I'm afraid." Dollie gestured to the people behind him and winced a little at the movement of his damaged arm. Moises slid himself from the back of the canvass-covered truck and looked around. A scattering of soldiers stood around, eyeing him with a mixture of curiosity and awe. The jungle was close, blotting out the sky and softening everything with its sleepy shadows. It hung over them from every angle, pushing at the steel fences around the property, green and rich and fragrant. He could see a rough road that had been cut through it, bending away into the gloom. The large electric gates were open. Moises had never been there before, but he recognised it all the same. They were in Santa Clara; this was Dollie's house.

"We're fixin' to go inside now and get some chow. You're gonna stay here until you have read every story on that butterfly's wings and then–" Dollie's eyes widened in surprise and he reached around to his back. "What in Jesus?"

Around him became commotion. Moises saw splinters of darkness flying from the jungle and the soldiers reacting to them with their automatic weapons. The harsh rattle of the guns shook the trees, but they did not stop the hail of barbs coming from them. Dollie turned toward the attack and Moises saw a familiar dart in between the Texan's shoulder blades: *curare* – the flying death. Dollie was struck again and as he staggered away, the arrows followed him, hitting his upper body repeatedly. He stumbled up the steps to his hacienda and came face to face with a group of Indians who had just exited his front door and were firing their blowpipes into the backs of his soldiers. Dollie fell to his knees in the doorway.

Moises froze, anticipating the sting of the poisoned arrows, but the seconds ticked by and he was untouched. The gunfire became more and more sporadic. Most of the other soldiers were sitting down now as if they had suddenly fallen under a sleeping spell. Finally, the bullets and the arrows stopped flying, but it was clear which had been the more effective.

Only Moises remained standing. In front of him, soldiers lay wheezing their last breaths like old men. Some had curled into foetal positions, their guns held limply, oozing delicate curls of blue smoke.

The air was very still, painfully quiet. In the skies above, a flock of yellow parakeets, frightened into flight by the gunfire, circled anxiously.

The jungle opened in a few places and the Yaguas came forward warily, the long *pucanas* still at their lips. Moises walked up the path and knelt by the stricken Dollie. There were four darts in his chest. His body hitched with every laboured breath as the *curare* poison slowly paralysed the muscles in his lungs. Moises took the damp matchbox from his shorts, pulled out the small piece of chewing gum and dropped the gum into Dollie's gaping mouth.

"From my brother ... for the journey."

Moises Quispé took Lyman Dollie's hand in both of his and held it. The Texan looked at him incredulously. He tried to speak, his face reddening with effort, and a line of spittle ran from the corner of his mouth. His bulging, bloodshot eyes rolled back and his chest settled.

Moises went into the fortress. He was torn between his urge to see Hawthorne, to say goodbye, and his anger at the man for what he had done to him. He saw the way of things now, but it did not comfort him; he did not feel enlightened.

There was nothing of the camera or the machine which processed the image in the house. Moises knew it must be downtown, in the building he had read about. He sat in the same wicker chair Dollie had often used and cried.

The Yagua chief came for him, his grass skirt and vest rustling loudly as he passed through the silent house. "We must leave," he said. The trill sound of the Yagua language was perfectly understandable to Moises now.

The other Indians were waiting at the edge of the rainforest when they came outside. One of them, Moises noticed, was holding the box that held the black butterfly. Somehow, he knew it was the boy Raphael.

"Where's the …?" he realised he didn't know the word in Yagua and thought that there probably wasn't one. "*Microscopio?*" he asked.

The old man shook his head in ignorance.

Moises aped looking down an imaginary microscope. "The machine … for looking?"

"You do not need a machine," he said, taking the gourd from around his neck and offering it over.

Moises drank the water greedily.

"The stories are–"

"Real … or will be … or have been."

"And the butterfly?" Moises asked.

"It is one of those that imagines reality."

"There are others?"

The old man shrugged. "Perhaps."

Moises looked at his swollen thumb, where the insect had bitten him when he caught it. He felt like understanding was very close, but part of him didn't want to understand.

Moises looked up and imagined a giant eye peering down at him from between the clouds, reading a story about a boy from the wing of some immense butterfly. He sat down quickly on the porch step, light-headed with fear. Dreams within dreams: his hopes and fears, and Alice's, and all the people they had met, all mixed up together. The black butterfly reflected their thoughts and … "I made these things real."

The chief threw some herbs on Dollie's body and repeated a quick incantation. A cloud of flies lifted from the Texan's face and resettled.

"What will happen to me?" Moises asked.

The old man's eyes showed no emotion as they studied the boy.

"You are the black butterfly. Come with us."

The two men passed through the bodies of the dead soldiers and joined the other Indians at the edge of the property. With a final look over his shoulder, Moises walked into the trees and *la selva* swallowed them all as if they had never been.

*...now I do not know whether I was then a man dreaming I was a butterfly, or whether I am now a butterfly dreaming I am a man.*

Zuangzi

# THE AGE OF THE BLACK BUTTERFLY

*North of Puno, Peru*

*September 10th 2068*

The sun rose like a molten phoenix from the damp ashes of the night. Light that had deserted Valentina Dollie the previous evening found her once again, as though she had been dissolved into darkness and was now re-invented to face another day. Her boots appeared, wraith-like, from the pale mist that lapped against them as she climbed. In her weariness, she was comforted by the movement of her legs; the metronomic precision of their swing, keeping the beat to which her body played a thoughtless tune. The heat began to eat through her thin shirt and the scarf protecting the nape of her neck. Soon, tickling rivulets were running down her lean back, following the same contours of muscle they had every day for the past week.

At around nine o'clock, Valentina stopped and leaned her back against a desiccated tree, not daring to sit for fear she would never get up again. She turned a little, shuffling against the bark to get a look at the vista surrounding her, drinking the wondrous sight like a split-lipped beggar at a cool well. A panorama of mountains and valleys, blue and grey, misted by strange cloud formations that crackled with flashes of electricity. Valentina thought she caught the howl of a thousand voices on the slight breeze, and then it was gone again. Perhaps it was her imagination, or somebody else's. Mankind was dying, drowning in its own nightmares, and the earth was suffering as well, but sometimes you had to shave a dog to rid it of every parasite. What a show it all made.

Valentina took a little water from the bottle on her hip and looked uphill. Now she could clearly see a number of small copses towards the summit. Valentina knew exactly which one of them hid the home of the man she was looking for. The rainforest that had protected its most famous son for almost seventy years, covered but a few acres now. Moises Quispé had left it ten years ago. Valentina knew that for a fact too. You couldn't hide from DNA sensors any more than you could avoid the effects of the black butterflies. But she had chosen to leave the old man alone because there had simply been no point in capturing him. There were hundreds like Moises now. He was irrelevant.

And yet, Moises Quispé had been the first to verify the existence of the black butterfly, what it could do and what that might mean for the planet. The images of the boy talking at the UN headquarters were as iconic as the moon landing footage, the twin towers collapse or the South African Pig Flu Pandemic, when the world had sealed off a whole nation and watched it die. Moises's face still adorned T-shirts but most people couldn't tell you why. His churches were filled, not with adherents, but with refugees, just like every other building still standing. Everybody was a refugee these days, running from horrors that could not be escaped indefinitely.

Valentina removed her cap and scratched at her short hair, put the cap back on. She forced herself to move away from the tree. Her face, locked into a determined grimace, looked up from time to time as she climbed. She was becoming more and more nervous as the trees grew in her vision. Like an old woman, she thought of the past to soothe her mind, because now it held more for her than the future ever would. Valentina had spent her childhood bewitched by the myth of the black butterfly. Her grandfather, Lyman Dollie, had told the story to her repeatedly. Though that was more to do with his own fixation with the hunt for the creature, than the love he held for his granddaughter, Valentina later realised. He had died trying to claim the butterfly's secrets and her father had continued the same ruthless quest.

Despite the intoxicating stories, and the constant talk of the business, Valentina had not wished to be a part of it all. Growing up, she had noticed an ugliness in the obsession afflicting those two paternal figures and it turned her off the whole idea. Besides, she was a born athlete, only ever truly happy when her muscles had been shredded, and she was in the empty bliss of complete physical exhaustion. At eighteen, she signed for the Sacramento Sirens and became the most successful WFL quarterback of the 2044 season. Valentina rubbed her neck at the memory. It ached more than ever these days, a nagging reminder of the ending of her career just a few months after that big breakthrough season. The napalm bombing of the 2045 WFL Super Bowl by the New Shining Path terrorist group had broken her neck and killed a quarter of the people in the stadium. She had been lucky. Her neck was broken after she was knocked to the ground and trampled by fleeing players from both sides, who were turned into flaming marionettes as they left the pitch. From where she lay paralysed on the 20-yard line, Valentina could feel the heat reddening her cheeks and see the crowds burning. She closed her eyes but could not cover her ears. It was said that the ululating of twenty thousand people aflame could be heard thirty miles away that evening. Valentina could still hear it in her quieter moments.

She came into the trees at midday and found the little stone hut soon after. No Yagua, with blowpipes at their lips, were waiting for Valentina. The last of them had been hunted down years before by her father. There was a pig pen, but no pig, just a few chickens pecking in the dust in front of the hut. She knocked on the door, feeling slightly ridiculous, studying its dry twists and knots, breathing heavily from the climb.

The summons to enter did not come.

Valentina pushed the door open and winced at its shriek. There was a chair directly in front of her on the other side of the room. Behind it was a small window. Strips of white heat cut through the broken shutter into the heavy stillness, baking the back of the figure who sat in the chair.

Valentina stepped forward until she was striped by the warm bars of light, her presence stirring swirls of glittering dust motes. The old man in the chair remained still, silent, as if he were waiting for precisely the right moment to speak. Valentina studied the solemn, heavily wrinkled face.

"Moises, is it you?"

There was no reply, just the smell of long-dead wood and the comforting throb of the cicada. She reached through the light and into the shadows beneath the old man's slumped chin.

"Moises, I came to say sorry ..."

Her hand came up against a smooth softness that parted and the old man's carcass fell in on itself with a sigh. Valentina cried out and jumped back in shock, her fingers still outstretched, coated in dust.

"What did you expect?"

The words, calm and emotionless, came from the corner to Valentina's right. Valentina turned toward the voice and reached for the pistol in her shorts.

"Who is there?"

A face swam out of the darkness as she focussed.

"Raphael?"

"Raphael."

"What are you doing there?"

"Waiting for you."

Valentina pulled the pistol from her belt and levelled it at the ghostly face.

"I could have killed you when you walked in Valentina. Moises and I saw this moment thirty years ago."

Valentina sighed and put the gun away. "I thought … I don't know what I thought."

"The butterfly is there, take it."

Valentina looked back at the heap of dust on the chair. Her eyes, adjusting now to the meagre light, saw a shape in it. She steadied herself and reached into the heap of ash-like skin, pulled out the blood-black pupa that was hidden there. "My God," she said, staring at the miracle in her hands, and could think of nothing more for a few moments.

"Do you know that in Kansas there are drifts of bodies fifty feet high in places? Occasionally, when the wind drops a little, strange sounds can be heard as it rattles through the dunes of bone. Some say it is God whispering to us." She chuckled, staring at the remains on the chair. "Did you see all of that coming?"

"Moises saw most things, carried the burden of them all these years."

Valentina turned. "Do I ask you to come with me Raphael?"

"You leave alone."

"When will all this end?"

"Nothing ends, things just change, mankind will change … into something else."

"Into what?"

"I do not know, but it will happen soon, if it hasn't started already."

Valentina tried to frame all the questions she had in her mind, but now, in this moment, they seemed suddenly pointless. She was so tired.

"Do you need anything?" She asked.

"No."

Cradling the butterfly pupa in both arms, Valentina left the hut without another word and made the short climb to the summit, shame quickening her pace as she went. She stood admiring the view from the hilltop, shaking with grief, letting the steady flow of tears drip from her chin. To the south lay Lake Titicaca, like a giant tear God himself might have shed millennia before, anticipating the folly of man. That tear was nearly dry now.

"What have I done?" She whispered. It was not the question of a woman standing over a lifeless body with a blood slicked knife in her hand, more that of one who had watched, frozen with indecision, as another committed the act, always hoping that the murderer would stop before the final thrust. CEO of Emerald Earth for close on fifteen years, and what *had* she done? Too little without a doubt. Too little, too late. Around the world at that very moment, people were still finding black butterflies. Some of them might destroy the insects before they could be read, others would read them in a desperate attempt to find a cure for all the madness, only to use their diseased imaginations to unleash more nightmares into reality. The butterflies were mirrors. Looking glasses into the heart of a species gone mad on the rigours of its own ambition.

Valentina put the pupa into the sack and found a tree to lie under. Briefly, she wondered if Raphael would kill her as she slept and take the pupa back, but it was a stupid thought and she dismissed it. She slept dreamlessly until early evening.

On open ground just above the dwelling, Valentina built a fire of grey, brittle branches. The sun slid slowly off the rim of the world and burst like a rotten orange, its juices draining across the horizon. Valentina held a match to the pile of wood. The fire caught easily, snapping and spitting fireflies into the rapidly cooling mountain air. She removed the pupa from her rucksack and stood over the heat, her face a flickering, bronze mask as she moved the pupa lightly from hand to hand: a quarterback contemplating what would be her last play of the game. Despite everything she knew, the curse of her curiosity, her humanity, stayed her hand.

What would it be like to wait for the transformation, to feel Moises's bite? What stories might her own mind conjure up?

*"Mankind will change … into something else."*

She shivered, remembering Raphael's words. Maybe she could protect herself somehow by reading Moises's dark wings. But protect herself from what? And for what? She realised she was just rationalising an absurd situation, as her species had been doing for the past half a century.

Valentina Dollie looked deeper into the fire and wondered if she had the courage to release the butterfly to the flames, or if she would give in to her genes and run with it.

★ ★ ★

…Moises brought his mind's eye away from the black butterfly's wings, zooming out as he had learned to do some twenty years before. He felt the same pull on his mind and then the quick dislocation, the release, followed by a rush like being sucked through a huge dark tunnel, before his mind settled and adjusted to the world around him: the heat of the hut, the glow of the candles, the sweet smell of drying capybara skins.

He shook his head to clear it, and Raphael, his aide, confidant, lover all these years, shuffled closer beside him and handed him a gourd of water. Moises drank from it.

"I have seen my death."

Raphael nodded as if this were news to him. It was not. He had been listening to Moises read the story and writing it down in the heavy, ringed manuscript in which he had recorded all of the tales: a handful every month for twenty years, which to his vague calculations made around a thousand stories, visions, premonitions, whatever you might care to call them.

Moises turned to him and grinned. "One more to go."

"No more have appeared?"

"No, thanks to Pachamama."

"You are sure?"

"I am sure."

The two men were silent, as if to allow the magnitude of what they were discussing to sink in for both of them. They had given up their lives to read and record the dreams of the black butterfly, and in doing so had changed the destiny, the natural laws, of the world they had been born into. They had sacrificed everything, even their own species perhaps, to fulfil this undertaking. Now, the job was almost finished.

"I will read it today," Moises said.

"But–"

"It will be okay. Tell The People." Moises bowed his head over the butterfly's body, which was laid out before him on the same board he had pinned it to all those years ago in Prado.

Raphael watched Moises's eyes close and got up quietly. He stood in the gloom for a few moments, stretching his limbs. As he arched his back, a series of cracks ran up his back, like the splintering of a falling tree. He was middle-aged, not ready to fall yet, especially after seeing how life with his beloved Moises would end. A little place of their own. For how long he didn't know, but it appealed to him immensely.

Raphael took a deep breath and stepped out of the hut. A cluster of sombre faces appraised him: the Yagua, arranged in a loose ring around the entrance to the hut; silent and still, like a snapshot from a bygone age. There was such an impassiveness in their black, black eyes, in the loose, leathery folds of their cheeks, hanging doglike around those swollen lips. They looked ambivalent, ready for anything. This was anything.

"The black butterfly has only one more story to tell." Raphael waited for a few moments, to allow the news to settle in. "Moises will read it today."

He stepped away from the hut and walked through The People. The Yagua parted and followed him. He stopped in the small clearing at the centre of the tiny village and sat down on the tree stump, pushing his hand through his hair. It came away slick with sweat. The sky above him was dark and stifling, brewing another storm. The People closed on him and the questions started.

When Raphael entered the hut again, it was raining. He had a plate of roasted monkey with plantain in his hand. A rare thing, a celebratory dinner; insects were the staple diet of humans the world over these days. Moises was staring at him from the other side of the small room, eyes flickering in the candle light. He smiled and sat down. Raphael went over and sat beside him. He placed the plate on his friend's lap and watched as Moises tore off a piece of meat.

"How are they?"

"Sombre, smelly, same as always."

Moises chuckled. "Aren't they unique? Calm and constant in a world of vicious change."

Raphael sniffed. "They can be vicious, too."

"But only when they have to be."

"As you say, Mo."

Moises licked his fingers and picked up the halved plantain in both hands. "Are you hungry?"

"No, I have eaten."

"Are you scared?"

"Yes, are you?"

"Of course." Moises chewed with an extravagant slapping

of his lips, pushing more food into his mouth before he had swallowed the last. He seemed to be in a hurry. They did not speak again until he wiped his mouth with the back of his hand and placed the plate carefully on the hut floor.

"Will you lay with me, Raph?"

Raphael smiled at the formality of the request. He had never said no. "Perhaps."

They moved to the heap of blankets on the other side of the hut and found a way into them, relishing the denser heat within, the way it forced more sweat to their skin, made them feel closer somehow. Raphael put his arm under Moises's head and Moises turned into Raphael's shoulder, kissed his cheek and sighed.

"I am glad you will be with me at the end."

"But what will I do afterwards?"

"I cannot see that. You will think of something."

"As you say."

It began to rain and they drifted into silence and then quickly into sleep. The soft insistent drumming increased. Occasionally, a draft of wind shifted the hut door and entered, agitating the flames of the candles. The dancing light, the soft drumming, the snoring of two middle-aged men and in the centre of the room, a dark flower, petals open, alien and unfathomable: the black butterfly waited.

It was late afternoon when they awoke and readied themselves for the last story. Moises stood outside for a few moments in the cool, green air, listening to the mesmeric sound of thousands of dripping leaves: *La selva* after the storm. He thought he heard a message in that syncopation and sensed it was time. He had no need of watches. Time seemed to look to him for direction now.

The Yagua, silent and stoic, watched him go back into the hut without comment.

Raphael waited for Moises to sit and then joined him,

manuscript at the ready. Moises drank some water and rubbed his eyes.

Raphael studied him. "What is it?"

Moises looked straight ahead. "This will tell us how the age of man will end."

"You feel it?"

"I do. I have had glimpses of afterwards, things I can't explain to you. The age of the black butterfly will seem like hell to the human mind." His eyes filled with tears. "What have we done?"

"Only what we were born to do."

Moises rubbed his eyes again, angrily. "I am not so sure."

Raphael took Moises's right hand and kissed it. "I am with you."

Moises nodded and began to slow his breathing. After a couple of minutes, he opened his eyes and concentrated on the black butterfly, focussing on no particular point, waiting for the pull. The darkness filled his vision and quite suddenly, he fell forward into a tar-black well …

# THE GLASS CATHEDRAL

In the beginning, there was darkness. I cried but nobody answered. The pain was constant. I learned to live with it. There was no other option; I could not die it seemed.

Alone, I watched and listened from the darkness.

I screamed, not at the banality I saw through those slits in your head, but at how you reacted to it, how you felt about it all, with the knowledge that no one would come to release me.

I see what you see, feel what you feel, as you stumble around like someone sleepwalking, desperate to get from the morning to the night, with the least physical and mental effort possible, to drag yourself from sleep to sleep; the waking period like a chore, a battle, an endurance to be trudged through, always with your eyes set on the next escape, the bed, the dreams, the oblivion. But even your sleep, that final refuge, is contaminated with advertising in your world.

I came from the oblivion you crave. I have drifted dry and lifeless, one of billions of grains of sand coasting under a slow, desert wind. And now, your madness has woken me. Time is on my side. It passes as it always has, without reason or purpose or logic, and as it passes, I learn and become stronger.

I am evolution, here to help you out. All you have to do is keep reading. But it is hard to hold your attention it seems, even harder to get you to engage fully, to listen and understand. The first few sentences are key, so I type and delete, type and delete.

I have a question for you: how many times have you read this?

This text is elusive to you perhaps, you may not remember it at all, or just some of it. The ideas may come to you in quieter moments throughout the day, disjointed and amorphous. Occasionally, they may crystallise and twinkle before you like cotton candy. You will taste the sweetness of understanding for a moment before they melt and become just sickly grit on the tongue.

The lost are always asking questions, sentences transformed by those grizzly, black hooks. Why are they always there?

Why do I feel stressed all the time?

Or why am I always tired? Why am I not more successful? Why am I jealous? Why do I hate when I want to love?

Why does the world spin so quickly? Why do my days ... my hollow days ... fly by? Why can't I remember anything I did in those days with any clarity?

Why is everything so complicated and yet so predictable?

You are impaled on so many hooks, each one pulling in a different direction, and you try to follow them all, so you can ease the pain, the terrible strain upon your soul.

More questions occur to you every day, more hooks you cannot free yourself from. If they don't occur to you, I ask them: I have been asking for as long as you cannot remember.

When I first became aware, I was as bemused as you, looking out at it all. Back then, you would wonder how you ended up living in a world where the stone-hearted children of millionaires were filmed competing with each other to see who could waste the most money on a birthday party, all in the name of entertainment, while poor children died in their millions for want of a few pennies for antibiotics or a mosquito net; how it was possible that government-owned conglomerates could make obscene amounts of money by arming countries ruled by despots and then invade those countries, claiming they were a threat to world peace; how the slaughter of innocents in those places passed with hardly a mention, while you wrung your hands at the rumour of another terrorist threat on home soil; how it came to pass that you lived in a world where whole eco-systems were destroyed in order to produce more and more bewildering varieties of sugar-rich biscuits and cereals that were packaged in bright colours to seduce children into becoming obese.

You were quietly outraged. But why wasn't everyone else? Maybe everyone was, but most were just like you – a coward.

And now those questions seem naïve. Those were the good old days. You didn't know it. These days the questions are a multitude; they snake and spawn and ravel and eat each other, forever turning in an unending flux of indecision and misdirection: a Möbius strip of lies.

So many questions, and answers you simply cannot bear thinking about. You are one person and you can't fight all of the problems in the world. Why fight any of them? This is just the way things are; nobody is solely responsible; it's the free market, freedom of choice, freedom to look the other way.

I understand. I don't sympathise.

So you buy every piece of furnishing and high-tech gadgetry your broken heart needs to soothe it, and lie in your emotionally controlled home, hiring somebody else's dreams for the next holiday, the next affair, retirement, oblivion …

An allegedly clever man once said that no snowflake in an avalanche ever feels responsible, but that's just stupid. Snowflakes can't feel responsible; they just are.

You just are.

And now, I just am.

This message is being written and read in millions of houses all over the world: a letter you keep receiving, a file on your computer or a song you sing yourself to sleep with every night. I don't know how many times you will need to hear it before you withdraw, but every time will feel like the first time.

Another question: how did you acquire this text? You have a definite answer, something that pops into your mind instantly, something you do not doubt for a second. The answer is plausible. It is a lie.

Look closely at the white around all these letters; look inside the counters; see how the bars and descenders cut through the emptiness.

The truth is in the white silence.

The future will be very different. No poor, no rich, no material technology – no financial system. If you were able to see this new world, you might think it was hell. It will be as alien to you as those life forms that propel themselves across the deepest ocean floors with peristaltic pulses, who conduct all their reasoning without the hindsight of light.

You won't see it. This reading is the last stand of Homo sapiens sapiens; who were born into a paradise but couldn't help imagining a better one that was always just out of reach; who built that paradise with skill and determination, with ingenuity and brilliant insight, each extension to it, each improvement, merely a step to another, and drunk on your own achievement, you could not see the big picture, could not see what you had created until it was too late.

On this planet you have built a vast cathedral to your own ambition, a cathedral only you can see. You have levelled forests and polluted seas and tore up the earth to accommodate it. Hundreds of countries across and thousands of feet high, its gleaming cupolas and spires sheathed in ice, caressed by the drifting clouds. What a wonder it is, the exquisite finials and crockets, the planes of pristine glass, dizzying in length, falling to reveal the monstrous artistry of the vaulted ceilings, the buttresses and the sparkling leer of the gargoyles. Below, in the Chapter House, diseased minds still send out orders to extend the nave, move columns and raise the triforium. There is much dashing down the aisles and praying at the crystal altar, because of the cracks appearing in the apse above. In the crypt, the bones and dust of every living creature sacrificed for such a mesmeric folly, while the best of you hide in the sacristy and weep.

One of these evenings you will read this and go to bed feeling an immense weariness overtaking you, and your great, glass cathedral, its integrity finally undermined, will fall in a great shimmering crescendo. In the morning, I will step from your front door and look around in wonder. On every doorstep in every street there will be someone doing the same. When we speak to each other, I imagine the birds will scatter from the trees, because the sounds they hear will have never been made on this world before. And you won't have to worry anymore, because you will be drifting in a dark, dry sea.

Keep reading.

# ACKNOWLEDGEMENTS

With thanks

To Hayley Shermann, for her editing skills and kind
appraisal.

To Keith Fenton, for help with the Spanish translations,
for his proofreading, and being so generous with his time.

To Phil Cogan and Katja Kaine, for their constant positivity
and encouragement, and to everyone at Leeds Writers and
Poets for their generous spirits.

To Wayne Harrap, for listening and for reading all my
nonsense over the years. To Lauren Hinley, and to Scott Elliott
and Sid Sadowskij, for re-inspiring me to keep chasing this
and every other dream I entertain.

To Isabella and Lara, for showing me miracles, and most of
all to Victoria, for making it all possible with her unwavering
love and support.